THE
NASTY
GNOMES

FOR JOHN —
EMPEROR OF THE F.E. —
GNASTY, GNASTY!

12.22.08

OTHER FICTION BY ROBERT REGINALD

If J.F.K. Had Lived (aka *The Attempted Assassination of John F. Kennedy: A Political Fantasy*) (as "Lucas Webb", 1976 & 1982)

Codex Derynianus (with Katherine Kurtz) (1998)

Katydid & Other Critters: Tales of Fantasy and Mystery (2001)

The Dark-Haired Man; or, The Hieromonk's Tale: A Romance of Nova Europa (2004)

The Exiled Prince; or, The Archquisitor's Tale: A Romance of Nova Europa (2004)

Codex Derynianus II (with Katherine Kurtz) (2005)

Quæstiones; or, The Protopresbyter's Tale: A Romance of Nova Europa (2005)

**The Phantom's Phantom:* A Novel of the Phantom Detective Agency* (2007)

Invasion! or, Earth vs. the Aliens: A Trilogy of Tales Inspired by H. G. Wells's Classic SF Novel, War of the Worlds (2007)

SELECTED NONFICTION BY ROBERT REGINALD

Reference Guide to Science Fiction, Fantasy, and Horror (as "Michael Burgess", with Lisa Bartle) (1992 & 2002)

**Xenograffiti: Essays on Fantastic Literature and Other Divers Topics* (1996 & 2005)

Murder in Retrospect: A Selective Guide to Historical Mystery Fiction (as "Michael Burgess", with Jill H. Vassilakos) (2005)

**Classics of Fantastic Literature; or, Les Épines Noires: Selected Review Essays* (with Douglas Menville) (2005)

Trilobite Dreams; or, The Autodidact's Tale: A Romance of Autobiography (2006)

*=Published by Borgo Press/Wildside Press

THE NASTY GNOMES

A Novel of *The Phantom Detective Agency*

As Taken from the Case Files of
Richard Curtis Van Loan, The Phantom

by

ROBERT REGINALD

Author of *The Phantom's Phantom*

Wildside Press, LLC
Rockville, Maryland

MMVIII

FIRST EDITION

10 9 8 7 6 5 4 3 2 1

CONTENTS

For

JOHN WEEKS AND WILLIAM MALTESE,

Two of the Gnastiest Gnombres in Town

And for

ARDATH MAYHAR

One of the Gnicest

PROLOGUE

THE PHANTOM RETURNS

▲

The poor old Past,
The Future's slave.
                    —Herman Melville

▼

REDLANDS, CALIFORNIA
29 JANUARY 2006

"Ah, my dear Professor Simmons," Dastrie Lee Underhill said, "We've been expecting you."

* * * * * * *

My name is Rob Simmons. I'm an emeritus professor of history at the local State U. I'd been actively employed there for thirty-five years until just a month ago, when I suddenly received an extraordinary legacy. My great-uncle Percy left me his entire fortune of two hundred million dollars—that was crazy enough!—but along with everything else, I also was given a set of his unpublished manuscripts.

My reclusive relative had apparently spent much of his life recording the exploits of his old friend, The Phantom Detective. But despite having published most of these accounts in long-forgotten pulp magazines, Uncle Percy also left a number of narratives that had never seen print, many of them dealing with the life and career of Richard Curtis Van Loan (a pseudonym!) *after* he supposedly retired in 1953.

I decided to rework and publish these fictions, beginning with *The Phantom's Phantom*—and I tried at the same time to verify the facts by doing some research of my own. But, try as I might, I could find very little corroborating evidence for any of the events or per-

7

sons described therein. Uncle Percy had been careful to efface his tracks.

According to him, The Phantom had established a corporation in November of 1953 to continue his work in the future. Surely there must be some trace of that organization, if it still existed—if it ever existed! But I could find nothing in the corporation or agency records of a Phantom Detective Agency, either in California or New York. Perhaps, I thought, perhaps the best-laid plans of Phantoms or men had come to naught. Perhaps—perhaps—I was just chasing another phantom.

But then I spotted a listing in the yellow pages under "Investigators & Investigation Svces." for PDA, Ltd., with a Fifth Street address in Redlands. Could this possibly be what I was looking for?

I eat lunch everyday in downtown Redlands, or occasionally in Mentone Beach. One of my haunts is Amando's Hideaway, a scrumptious Mexican restaurant that served an absolutely searing cauldron of *caldo de siete mares* soup, among others. I plopped myself down into my usual corner booth, and spent an hour, in between sips of the fantastic, fiery broth, gazing across the street at the upstairs corner office, deciding what to do next. No one entered or departed the structure other than the omnipresent pigeons (the rats of the bird world), roosting and cooing in the quaint window alcoves above me. I saw no lights behind the drawn blinds. The place might as well have been abandoned for all I could tell.

Finally I made up my mind, and asked for the check. I crossed the street and walked up the plain stairs to a second-story office. I opened the old wood door and entered the room. Three individuals sat facing me behind a long mahogany table. The one in the middle was a slim, silver-haired lady of perhaps seventy-five or eighty.

She stared at me with her intense green eyes, and then she smiled.

"Ah, my dear Professor Simmons," she said, "We've been expecting you. Please have a seat."

The office was lined with oak bookshelves that had obviously been constructed *in situ*. It was all I could do to restrain myself from examining the volumes arranged thereon.

"What is this place?" I asked.

"Please sit down," she repeated, pointing to the lone empty chair in front of the desk.

I complied.

"I was pleased to read *The Phantom's Phantom*."

"But it's not even published yet," I said.

I had just been correcting proofs earlier in the day.

"Nonetheless, it's a good beginning. We want to see you continue with your literary career."

"Who's 'we'?"

"Well, you obviously know—or think you know—who *I* am," she said. "My colleagues shall remain nameless for now. Not that it matters much. We're all *noms* of someone else's *plume*, you know!"

"I wondered about that," I muttered to myself. "I mean, really: Dastrie?! It sounds like a Faustian bargain with a brand name."

"I rather like it," the lady said. "I think it suits me. It's what Richard called me, and I'd be fond of it for that reason alone. I do believe I'll keep it!"

She laughed out loud then, the sound of chimes tinkling in the breeze of a summer's afternoon; and I realized for the first time the kind of hold she must have had on The Phantom Detective—or on any man, to tell you the truth. Even at her age, she could still charm and enchant and play the ingénue.

"You said you were expecting me," I said. "Then you must have some purpose for wanting me here."

"How very perceptive of you, Professor Simmons. Yes, indeed we do. What manuscript did you intend to tackle next?"

"Well, the next volume in chronological order is *Yelloweyes*, I believe. It's set in mid-1954."

"I remember that case," Dastrie said. "Yesss. But—there's a gap in the sequence, isn't there?"

"I wondered about that. It's over six months from the end of *The Phantom's Phantom* to the beginning of *Yelloweyes*. What happened in between?"

Dastrie Lee Underhill reached under the desk and pulled out two manila folders, each of them stuffed with faded, yellowing paper. She dropped them on the mat in front of me with a loud bang and a swirl of ochre dust.

"*This* is what happened," she said. "*This* is what we want you to write."

I leaned over and picked them up. One was labeled *The Nasty Gnomes* and the other *The Zero Zombies*. I started paging through the manuscripts, and then looked up in surprise.

"But, but, these names are…," I said.

"*Yes!* That's why these have been kept hidden for so long, even from your Uncle Percy. Such a dear man, but not always very quick on the uptake. Given the recent history of our country, it's time that they be revealed to the public.

"You'll be the one to make The Phantom return to life in all his glory. Never did he encounter such a vicious set of criminals. Never was he so pressed to solve a mystery. Never did he undertake such risks.

"I know. I was there. I saw the stories unfold.

"It began while we were still battling *The Phantom's Phantom* in California, although we didn't know it at the time. It was only after we returned to the Big Apple...."

CHAPTER ONE

COMES THE DARK
▲

The sun's rim dips, the stars rush out:
At one stride comes the dark.
                              —Samuel Taylor Coleridge
▼

NEW YORK, NEW YORK
MONDAY, 14 DECEMBER 1953

Darkness.

Night filled my soul as I stalked my prey. It cloaked me in its ebon garb—black coat, dark hat, a scarf of inky tentacles wrapping itself 'round the jaw-line of my face—as I slinked silently down the street, ducking into door- and alleyways, avoiding the light, keeping just far enough behind to avoid being noticed.

Not that he *would notice! His arrogance bedazzled his sensibilities.*

He was looking for a girl, a black *girl, any* black girl, *someone weak and stupid and compliant to warm his bed for an hour or three. He prayed for female prey, not knowing that he himself was being hunted through the urban jungle.*

This was the man who'd altered my life forever, who'd robbed me of my upright father, my dear mother, my beloved sister. The law, the forces of supposed righteousness, had laughed when I'd tried to bring this fiend to justice. Not enough evidence, they'd said, to accuse such an upstanding scion of society. We'd be tossed out of court, they'd told me.

It wasn't right. It wasn't fair. It wasn't just!

But my heart had to fracture a second time before I could find myself again. And when I'd sloughed off enough of my humanity to

11

*contemplate an abyss unadulterated by fear, by love, even by hate—
then, and only then, was I ready!*

I became The Phantom of the night.

Now it was my *turn to kill—and his turn to die!*

*My gazelle was becoming nervous. Perhaps he'd heard the
hard-soled heel of my boot striking a cobblestone. He suddenly
turned around, gazing quickly back down the street where I was
shadowed within a well of silence. He saw only what I meant him to
see—nothing! Nothing but the night.*

At one stride comes the dark.

*The sounds of the city died slowly away, as if the alley cats, the
twitter-birds, the creepy critters that crawled from their gutters
when the sun went down, were all waiting for the beast to pass.*

*Another block—but even the dollar whores were safe within
their dollar-beds this evening. Not a creature was stirring, not even
a louse! Just an odd phantom or two.*

I waited. I watched. I pounced!

*"Who are you!" he demanded, when I confronted him with the
twin imperatives clutched in my black-gloved hands.*

"Richard Curtis Van Loan," I whispered.

"Van Loan! But...but...."

*"You murdered three of us," I said, "but left the fourth alone
with his grief. That was a* big *mistake, Maussey."*

"No," he said. "I beg you. I have money...."

"My money!" I said. "You have my *money, Peter. I don't want
my money now that it's been tainted by your soul. Keep my money, if
you can, when you pass through the gates of Hell. It won't buy you
much there."*

*Then I shot him twice in the head, and took his wallet and watch
and ring to make it look like a robbery. I threw them into a nearby
gutter.*

*And in my mind, I continued shooting him over and over and
over again, over and over....*

* * * * * * *

"Richard!"

Dastrie was shaking me awake.

I was soaked in sweat, still immersed in the nightmare of my
life.

"Richard!" she said again, this time more urgently.

"I'm OK," I finally said, sitting up in bed and panting my breath away.

It was a lie, of course: I would never be OK again.

"You need...."

"What?" I asked, shaking off the last threads of the night. I reached for the glass of water sitting on my nightstand, and gulped some of the cold liquid. "I need *what*?"

"You need to see...someone," she said. "These...these dreams are.... They're tearing you up inside. They're hurting us."

"And who would you suggest?" I said. "*Who*, Dastrie? Sigmund Freud? Alfred Adler? Dr. Jekyll? Mr. Hyde? Who can I trust with these fragments of myself? Who's safe enough?"

"I...I don't know," she finally said.

"No, you *don't*. You have no idea what I've been through."

"You could *tell* me," my wife said.

"No, I can't!" I blurted out. "You don't understand. You can't understand. These are things that must remain buried forever."

"Except they're *not* staying buried, Richard. You relive them every other night. You scream and yell and squirm—and you...you even kick me. I know you don't mean to, but you frighten me sometimes. How can I help? What am I supposed to do?"

"Leave me be," I said. I was angry at myself more than her. "Just let me alone, please."

Then I got up and slunk into the bathroom. I deliberately left the light off. I sloughed off my underwear and oozed into the shower. I turned the hot water knob as high as I could bear it. The black heat melted my miasma, soothed my nerves, and gave me strength to face another day.

But it wasn't the rosy-fingered Dawn that I sought.

Oh, no.

It was Darkness.

My old friend.

* * * * * * *

I had three appointments scheduled that afternoon, and none of them turned out as expected.

It was my first day back in the office. I'd spent nearly two months in California, initially to investigate the death of my friend, Frank Havens, and then to help Dastrie recover from the burns that Laurella McCarty had inflicted upon her; and then—well, and then to play in the sunshine of Southern California. I didn't want to go home—ever—but Dastrie's parents insisted on her return, and I had unfinished business to complete. I was not a happy camper, folks, on that second Monday in December.

My morning was overshadowed by the slings and arrows of my lovely wife, and by the piles of paperwork waiting for me. I was tired—God, I was worn—even before I began. Lizzie, whose patience surpassed that of Job, kept bringing me documents to sign, until finally I said, "Enough!"—and whisked her away.

After our argument that morning, Dastrie and I had both gone away angry, not for the first time; but I'd asked my secretary to arrange a lunch with her at The Marionette. We could bury our hatchets in the cheese rather than each other.

"Your father's coming to see me this afternoon," I said, sitting down across from her.

"Yes," she said, frowning slightly, while she smoothed her lipstick. "I don't think either Daddy or Mother appreciated being omitted from our wedding ceremony. He says we should have waited."

"At my advanced age, I couldn't have waited much longer," I said, trying to smile back at her. I was sick at heart about the words we'd had over my nightmare.

"At your advanced age, my dear," my wife stated quite succinctly, "You would have waited quite as long as necessary!"—which was, after all, only the truth. "But I didn't want to wait, and I told him that too. I also said that if he and Mother really wanted to throw some kind of celebration for us in the new year, well, I knew you wouldn't object. That quieted the old bear."

"That must be why he's meeting with me."

"I don't know, Richard: he said nothing to me about it when I talked to him this morning."

I was pondering her response when César delivered our roasted asparagus wrapped with prosciutto and drizzled with olive oil; it was mated with two halves of a freshly sliced and cored pear—light, tasty, and very satisfying indeed.

I speared a green spear with my fork, and savored the subtle mix of flavors. How utterly delicious!

"Then I wonder...?" I asked.

But not for long.

* * * * * * *

Former New York City Police Commissioner Teobaldo Eduardo "Fast Eddie" Underhill had suffered an almost-disgrace that had effectively ended his municipal career. He'd never been a beat cop, but had been grabbed by Mayor LaGuardia from his post as head of the Texas Department of Criminal Investigation, ostensibly to generate additional revenue streams for the NYPD. He'd survived and prospered until he'd finally stumbled over a scandal that even he couldn't hide, when one of his enemies tried to frame him for supposed misuse of funds.

His daughter and wife had come to me then and begged for my assistance, and I'd done what I could to salvage the family's honor and reputation, although Fast Eddie had gracefully exited "stage left" shortly thereafter.

That was my introduction to Dastrie Lee Underhill—and to Zenobia Underhill, her staid society mother.

"*¡Salud y pesos!*" the retired cop said, when Lizzie announced him, in a traditional Mexican greeting offering health and wealth to the recipient.

Fast Eddie was a decade older than me, but his gray hair, pronounced paunch, and sagging chin spoke volumes about his real age. He held out a callused, pudgy, splotchy hand (which I gladly took and shook), beaming his crooked smile back at me, his lone porcelain incisor flashing like a beam from a corkscrewed lighthouse.

"Hey, welcome to the corral, sonny. I was truly grateful that it was you who finally tamed our little filly. She was gettin' mighty rambunctious at times, takin' hold of the reins once too often. We was beginnin' to worry our heads off over her. Zennie Lee and me hope to arrange a little shindig next month to, well, you know—toast and roast the bride and groom—and then get roarin' drunk on good ole Texas tea!"

I chuckled. "Sounds good to me, 'Dad.' Just have Zenobia phone Dastrie, and they can arrange a schedule. I know the dear ladies will have us all properly lassoed and hogtied in right good order."

"I truly do think so," he said. "But that's not why I wanted to see you, Van. You follow any of the local news while you were gallivantin' all over California?"

"Not much," I said. "I was a tad busy with other things, as you may have heard. Haven't even seen a New York paper until this weekend, when we got back."

"Well, to step straight into the old pile of cow crappy, so to speak, we've been havin' a right ole time of it here—or rather, my pals on the Force have. There's been something *really* strange agoin' on in the Big City, *compadre*."

I sat up in my chair. Fast Eddie wasn't the type to become riled over minor issues, and if he'd been drawn back into departmental affairs on such short notice, the crisis must be serious indeed.

"What's happened?" I asked.

"Well, now, it started as a series of routine muggin's about the time you picked up stakes for the West Coast," Eddie said. "But... the attackers were all, well...they were all dwarfs!"

"You're kidding!"

"Not a bit. Five or six or seven of these damned pipsqueaks would trick someone into an alley by cryin' and carryin' on and all and beggin' for help—and then attack the victims, forcin' 'em at gunpoint to empty their pockets or purses. That's how it all started.

"At first we didn't pay much attention. Crime is common in the city, you know, and tourists are easy prey for the professional thieves and cons. But then they started gettin' rougher."

"Oh, come on, Eddie, surely you're exaggerating. They might have guns, sure, but how could these little people physically threaten anyone other than the weak and elderly?"

"That's what I thought too, when I first heard of it, but when Captain Sabatini showed me the case files, I got real antsy. Week by week, it just got worse, until the first of this month, when a banker who resisted handin' over his wallet was beaten to death by a dozen of these pica-goons. Don't ask me how they did it, but there ain't no question that they started right down at the man's feet—and then walked up his body with their sticks. They probably used metal pipes or somethin' like that. The coroner had a *real* hard time identifyin' what was left of his body.

"It's like they're all juiced up with somethin', Van. The guy who was attacked apparently gave as good as he got, at least at the beginnin'. The blood spatter says he may have even killed one of 'em—but no body was found, just drag marks.

"And there was another odd thin' too. The Natural History Museum was broken into last week, and one of the night watchmen was assaulted by the creatures—he survived to tell his tale. Then they busted into one of the exhibits and stole this big chunk of rock."

"A rock?"

"Yep, an asteroid or somethin' like that. Strange, ain't it?

"Anywho, they brought me in last week after the story leaked to the press. The Mayor put me in charge of a special taskforce to find and eliminate the 'Nasty Gnomes,' as the 'papers are callin' 'em.

"I truly need your help, Van. We're getting' nowhere real fast with this one, and the pressure from local businessmen is mountin' somethin' fierce. Another corpus was found this mornin'."

"How many does that make?"

"Five, we think. The little men are gettin' touchier and tougher with each attack. See, it's even startin' to affect the Christmas trade—no one wants to come downtown anymores. The merchants are screamin' their heads off at the City Council, and the City Council's at the Mayor, and the Mayor at the Commissioner, and, well, hey, you know the drill."

"I'm retired, Eddie."

"I know that, but you always got results, Van. We need somethin' to happen here real fast like. People won't shop if they don't feel safe. So I gotta live up to my name on this one."

"Fast Eddie, huh? I'll do what I can to help, you know that. You'll get me copies of the files?"

"I already brought 'em with me—Lizzie has everythin'. And thanks, Van, thanks so much for bein' there. I know you'll take right good care of my Dastrie Lee."

I shook his hand again. There weren't many left in the world like Fast Eddie Underhill—a man with a sense of honor and a heart of pure grizzle.

* * * * * * *

After I took a brief break, Lizzie brought me the documents she'd prepared to establish The Phantom Detective Agency, Ltd. in the State of New York. Everything appeared to be in order, but they still needed to be reviewed by my attorney, retired Judge Alger R. Wickizer. And, of course, I still had to assemble an East Coast crew to assist me—whenever I had the time and inclination. Since it appeared I was about to embark on a new challenge, sooner would perhaps be better.

Then Lizzie announced my next visitor, someone with the unlikely moniker of Washington Jefferson. He was a dark-skinned man of perhaps forty-five years. His face looked familiar somehow, but I couldn't place him.

"Mr. Jefferson?" I said, motioning him to the chair in front of me.

"Ah thanks you, sir," he said. He had a deep, gravelly voice that was measured in slow beats of patience and pain.

"You ain't hardly met me before, ah knows it, and ah does 'preciate you givin' me this time with you. My brother, he worked for you."

"Your brother?" Suddenly the light struck my brain. "You mean Roscoe? He was your brother? But his surname was Wallace."

"Yes, sir. His real name was Adams Jefferson. My Daddy, he named us seven young'uns after the You-Ess presidents: Washington, Adams, Madison, Monroe, Jackson, Lincoln, Grant, and Roosevelt. But Adams, he never liked his name, so he used 'Roscoe Wallace' instead."

"I was very sorry to hear of his death. He served me faithfully for many years. I made sure that your mother was well taken care of. I don't think he had any children."

"He never married, sir. Ah 'preciates your kindness, ah surely does, as do all my brothers. But that's not why ah takes the subway all the way down from Harlem just to come to see you. No, siree. My Roscoe, see, he was doin' your work whilst he was kilt."

"What are you talking about?" I asked. "Mr. Wallace maintained certain aspects of my office and household, but that was all. I never gave him any other assignments—and to give him his due, he never asked for any."

"Roscoe, he would have knelt before your chair, sir, he so admired you. He thought you was the greatest man he ever did meet. He wanted so much to be jus' like you. So when he finds something really wrong, and you were gone out to Californie, he takes it upon hisself to 'vestigate the 'sishuashon.' He says to me: 'Washington, somethin' evil's goin' on in Harlem, and ah has to find out what it is.' That's what got him kilt, ah knows it."

"What else did he tell you?"

"Ah tries to 'member, but it's hard. The month before he died, he had this girl, see, name of Ruby Diamond. She work in the club they call The Ebonesque. White folks, they go down there to 'sperience the jazz and booze and black-skinned babes. Ha! They don't know nothin' 'bout nothin'! But this Ruby, she knows somethin', all right, somethin' bad that got my Roscoe into big-time troubles. He used to call her his 'Ruby-Sill'."

"His *what*?"

"Ah dunno what it mean. But somethin'—it surely do mean somethin'. You gotta find out for me and my brothers, sir. Roscoe, he was a good man, and he done real fine by you. Please, sir, find out who kilt him, and let him sleep his sleep of peace."

"I promise that I'll do everything I can to find his killer and bring him to justice. But I can't do it alone. I need your help, Mr. Jefferson."

"What can *ah* do, sir? I's just a bus driver."

"You can help show me the way. You can open doors that wouldn't be accessible to me. You can come work for me."

"Work for *you*?"

"Yes. I can pay you more than the city does. And after we find your brother's murderer, I'll keep you on the payroll. I need someone who knows the undercurrents in Harlem, and who can help me track down the criminals there."

"Ah dunno, sir. Ah has to think about this, and talk to my missus. She may not like it."

"I understand. Take a day or two and get back to me, please."

"Ah thanks you, sir, and ah does 'preciate the offer. You're everythin' my brother said you were."

I stood up and extended my hand. Washington Jefferson hesitated a moment before taking it, and then he turned and exited the door.

I buzzed Lizzie, and asked her to request the case file on Roscoe's death from Fast Eddie Underhill. The former Commissioner owed me that much, at least.

* * * * * * *

My third appointment wasn't scheduled until four o'clock, so I took another break, this time heading for the roof. Some years past I'd had the structure renovated to provide a private entrance and exit to the building, and to erect a refuge from the world up on top, a place of privacy where I could retreat when things became too tense.

I'd created a kind of Japanese garden, with a greenhouse, gazebo, sculptures, and several walkways, and I found that I could shed almost any care with a few moments of wandering through the bushes. Even in the heart of winter, when the chill wind whips up the East River and freezes the very marrow of one's bones, I could still find warmth in my soul just by being there. I called it my "*wa*-cup."

I returned to my desk an hour later, and sipped some hot tea that Lizzie had fixed. I had no idea who the next gentleman was, and I didn't recognize him when he was announced.

"Mr. Van Loan," the man intoned. He was as young and sleek as a sea lion, with black, oily, smoothed-back hair that would remain plastered to his scalp even in the heart of a hurricane. He smelled of raw power. "R. M. Cohn."

I extended my hand. His flesh was cold and clammy, and I pulled back a little at the touch. "I have a note here saying that you've expressed interest in donating to the Van Loan Foundation?"

"Ah, yes, of course," he replied. He reached into the inside pocket of his tailored suit coat, and pulled out a slim piece of paper that he handed to me.

"That's quite, quite generous," I said, raising my eyebrows. "Ten thousand dollars will help educate many deserving students. You represent the Right Is Might organization? I don't think I've heard of that."

"You might say that I'm one of their agents," Cohn said. "You might say that our organization represents the best of what America has to offer. You might say that we want to shape the future of this fair country so that it can be the best that it can be. 'Right Is Might' is our slogan, and 'Right Is Might' is our rallying cry."

"Yours is a political group, then?"

"You might say that politics are involved, and you might say that religion is involved, and you might say that all decent things are involved. We want to make things better. We want to make the *people* better. But there are elements in the world, sir, elements within our own society, that are fighting to overturn the values on which America was based. For several years now, we've been active in promoting the good and decent things that America stands for, and battling those forces which stand against us.

"The junior Senator of Wisconsin is just one of the high-placed officials who supports our aims—one of many, I might add. But it's hard to fight the radical elements of the media without appearing unreasonable on occasion."

"I imagine so," I said.

"So we are looking to recruit soldiers for our army to help liberate America from the forces of evil, men and women who'll be willing to do whatever is necessary to combat the communists and liberals and weak-minded individuals that lurk around every corner. We thought that you might like to become such a fighter for freedom."

"I shall certainly give the prospect every due consideration," I said. "But you should know, Mr. Cohn, that we have a policy at the Foundation of never accepting money from organizations with a political agenda. So, with great reluctance, I'm forced to return your check to you uncashed."

I handed it back across the desk. He looked at me a long minute, as if not believing what had just occurred.

"Mr. Van Loan," he finally said, "you are either for us or against us. There is no middle ground in modern America. I urge you to reconsider my gift—and my offer."

I nodded my head up and down, very slowly and sagely.

"In the words of Stephen Crane, I would guess, then, that I'm just a toad," I said in very measured tones. "It's been interesting meeting you, Mr. Cohn."

He stood up abruptly when I rose in my chair.

"You'll regret this, Van Loan!" he blurted out, almost in spite of himself. "You'll...."

"Perhaps," I said. "But I certainly don't regret my decision right now."

I smiled and buzzed for Lizzie. When she appeared, I said, "Mr. Cohn was just leaving."

My smile faded quickly after he departed. Cohn was a dangerous man. I determined to find out more about him—and quickly. Then I stretched my sore back. I reached over and dialed Dastrie's number.

"Hey, woman," I said when she answered, "how'd you like a date with an older man?"

"I dunno," she said through the instrument. "Will you wine me and dine me and ravage me afterwards?"

"I might manage a steak sandwich and some coffee and a cheap flick at a cut-rate theater."

"OK, I'm easy. It's a date!"

And you know something: she was, too!

CHAPTER TWO

A DWARFISH THIEF

▲

Now does he feel his title
Hang loose about him, like a giant's robe
Upon a dwarfish thief.
— William Shakespeare

▼

NEW YORK, NEW YORK
MONDAY EVENING, 14 DECEMBER 1953

We dined that evening at Chez Grenouille, where the specialty of the house was the "flying frog legs" of master chef Lannie Frétillement. Dastrie preferred the "poached peach," however, with *pommes de terre en robe de chambre* (I called them "spuds in mud") and the *cobaye haïtien* (which I thought a bit, well, over-the-top; one might as well be eating hamster). I much preferred the *cuisses* (which "flew" because of their fiery spices) with *haricots verts*, my favorite green veggies, fixed with thinly sliced almonds snowflaked over the top. *Délicieux!*

Our table was semi-private—by choice—so I was able to bring my dear companion up-to-date on the latest developments.

"Oh, I've heard of Mr. Cohn," she said. "A thoroughly nasty piece of work. Don't you remember? We saw his dubious talents on display recently at those televised Congressional hearings, the ones investigating the so-called communists that were supposed to have infiltrated the government. If he had his way, Richard, all free-thinking men and women (especially the women!) would be locked away in concentration camps."

"Then we must do whatever we can to see that doesn't happen," I said. "But we have several issues pending that are somewhat more pressing."

"Yes, the 'Nasty Gnomes'—and Roscoe's murder. We need to start building an East Coast version of the PDA."

"I'll trust your organizational skills to begin the process of putting together an actual office—I want something distinct from the corporation. Meanwhile, I'll contact a few of my old friends, and see if we can set up a meeting in a day or two to review some possibilities."

After dessert—cherries jubilee—we decided to walk the six blocks back to the Brockleigh-Greeneleaffe Building, our temporary home. The night was clear and cold, with a light breeze whistling through the skyscraper canyons of near-downtown Manhattan. They were filled with the ghosts of Christmas past and present, highlighted by the gaudy decorations and flashing lights that lined the businesses to either side of the street.

"They're almost pretty," Dastrie said, her left arm entwined tightly in mine. "It's supposed to snow later in the week. I do love this time of the year."

"Gorgeous," I agreed, but I wasn't watching the displays. I thought to myself again how lucky I was to have taken this particular road in life.

"I talked to a Dr. Lichgram this afternoon. He specializes in dream therapy, and I thought…."

"No!" I said. "Absolutely not! We've already talked about this. I can't take the risk of revealing something that might be used against us. You need to understand, Dastrie, that I've done many things over the years that border on illegality. I have enemies. Surely dear Laurella taught you that lesson!"

Laurella was the sister of the Phantom's Phantom, Riley McCarty; I'd killed both of her brothers in the steam room beneath the Hot Springs Hotel in San Bernardino. She'd escaped—and we'd have to deal with her another time.

At this hour of the evening, the pedestrian traffic had finally begun to diminish, with most of the merchants already being shut down for the night. The holiday shoppers would return again tomorrow, I knew. We might just have been a couple of lonely travelers on the road to perdition, the click-click-click of our heels marking point-counterpoint in our headlong journey to hell.

As we passed an alleyway between two looming structures, I heard a noise.

"Help me!" a weak, high-pitched voice gasped. "Please help." It might have been a woman or a child.

We both stopped dead in our tracks.

"Richard!" Dastrie said, "We must…."

"Stay here!" I ordered, and then slowly eased into the darkness, my hand feeling for my belt buckle as a precaution.

"Who is it?" I called out, letting my eyes adjust to the dim light. "What's wrong?"

A small mound huddled against one wall shifted position slightly, as if sitting up. I could see the outlines of several large trash barrels looming just behind her—but very little else.

"Help me!" she whispered again.

"What's wrong?" I repeated, straining to see who or what this was.

But I only received a whimper in reply. Something suddenly seemed very odd about this scenario.

I was starting to retreat when they surged out of the shadows, a swarm of small figures darting and dashing this way and that. Something metallic struck my right shin calf, and I staggered under the impact.

"Richard!" Dastrie screamed.

"Stay back!" I yelled, both to her and my assailants, pulling a derringer out of my buckle. I instinctively cocked one barrel, and when I was attacked again, aimed and pressed the trigger at the nearest figure. I heard one of them scream in pain.

But nothing seemed to stop the little monsters. I shot a second time, wounding or killing another, and then dropped the gun to the ground. I pulled a slender blade from under my belt, and whipped it at the little men.

Another couple of strikes against my legs brought me level with the filthy floor of the alley, my fine clothes being soiled by the trash of the Big City—and although I sliced and diced deeply into the bodies of several of my attackers, I knew that I was doomed to lose this particular battle in the end. There were just too many of them: they would either kill or severely injure me.

Is this how The Phantom meets his end? I found myself thinking.

Then the shots rang out—one-two-three-four-five!—and my assailants began careening around me like bowling pins. A second set of five bangs, each of them carefully measured and utterly deadly, drove the creatures back into the recesses of the unending shadows.

Suddenly they were gone—just like that!

I could hear the sirens warbling in the distance as the police responded, and through the throbbing pain in my legs and abdomen, the last thing that I recalled before falling into a deep, dark dream was Dastrie throwing her arms around me, while simultaneously banging me on the head accidentally with her pearl-handled .22.

* * * * * * *

I awoke a few hours later in St. Victor's Sanitarium, a small private hospital catering to the upper crust. Dastrie was dozing in a chair to one side, but she immediately stirred to life when I tried to raise myself up—and found myself involuntarily groaning with the pain.

"Don't move!" she said. "You're covered with bruises."

"Any...anything broken?" I managed to gasp.

"You may have cracked a rib or two, but everything else seems to be fairly intact, much to the surprise of your doctors. They're keeping you overnight for observation."

"As long it's no more than that," I said. "The 'Nasty Gnomes' have suddenly become personal. Oh, thank you, by the way, Mrs. Van Loan, for saving my worthless life."

"All in a night's work, sir!" she said, grinning. Her smile always made my world green. "I'm just glad they got the message: I was running out of bullets. The police will want to talk to you in the morning."

"Did they catch any of the dwarfish thieves?"

"Not a one, so far as I know," my wife said. "They just vanished, even their bodies. In the few seconds that it took me to reach you, everything just *evaporated*, Richard. I could hear the injured ones crawling away, gasping with the effort, and I think the rest were picked up and carried off by their brethren. I couldn't really see very well after dashing in from the fully-lit street—and I was more concerned about your safety than anything else. Surely we killed several of them."

"I don't know," I said. "They seemed remarkably agile, and extremely strong for their size."

I yawned, and suddenly realized just how tired I was.

"I'm going to sleep now. I've about run out of steam."

Dastrie bent down and kissed me on the lips, her fragrant tresses brushing against my face.

"Rapunzel, Rapunzel, let down your hair," I whispered from within my waking dream, grasping at any lifeline I could find.

CHAPTER THREE

THE FROG-PRINCE

▲

When you were a frog,
And imprisoned in the well!
　　　　　　　　—The Brothers Grimm

▼

NEW YORK, NEW YORK
TUESDAY, 15 DECEMBER 1953

Early the next morning, I had a visitor before I could even stir from my restless bed. My night had been filled with visions of ugly dwarfs brandishing pikes, and I hadn't slept well. My cuts and bangs throbbed and ached and prodded me with pains, reminding me of just how old and creaky I'd become. More than anything else I felt anger—a growing rage at how easily I'd been duped. Saved by a woman!—and even though she was *my* woman, the thought gnawed at the edge of my soul.

When Fast Eddie Underhill poked his head through my door at seven A.M., I was just finishing breakfast—two poached eggs, a slice of plain rye toast, and a glass of tomato juice—and Dastrie was there by my side, munching on an apple and slurping the black coffee she drank by the gallon.

"Commissioner," I said.

I tried to put aside my tray, but he had to help me.

The policeman folded his daughter in his arms. "So glad you're OK, Dastrie Lee," he said. Then he turned to me: "Hear you both had a rough-and-tumble evenin'. Now, Van, you can see just what we're facin'."

"They seem almost inhuman," I said.

"Yes sir, that's as good a word as any. Other survivors have all said how quick they are, how indestructible, how deadly. They move so very fast, and even when hurt, they just don't go down.

"They came through the walls, borin' holes in the plaster and bricks of the cellars. We think they use the tunnel system down under the city to travel. Most folks, they don't know how much stuff is located underground.

"Of course, we put our people down the shafts, but there's lots of places to hide. They didn't find nothin'.

"There's even a hoary old tale that *real* dwarfs from the Catskills once mined the caves beneath the city for coal and precious stones; if they caught you, they'd do the Texas two-step on you."

"Did you find any of the bodies?" I asked.

"Nope. Lots of blood sprinkled all over the damned alley, but no ruddy corpuscles. They must've carried 'em away with 'em. Oh, we found somethin' else there too."

"What?" I asked.

He handed me a grainy, black-and-white photograph of what appeared to be a graffito painted on the wall. It said:

> Bleed, my little goats, bleed,
> Or give me the Van Loan I need.

Etched beneath the words was a symbol of a lidless eye arrayed above a pyramid. It reminded me of the official seal of the United States of America.

"It was traced in blood," Fast Eddie said.

"So they were actually targeting me," I said. "It's comforting, in a way, to realize that there's an intelligence behind all this mayhem. It means that I have a new adversary out there, someone to fight and bring to justice, just like I've done in the past. One-Eye, indeed!"

"Perhaps," the former Commissioner said. "But it's too soon to go jumpin' off to conclusions. We haven't received any demands from the gnomes—and until we do, I can't tell you for sure that this was even left there by them."

"One thing's for certain," I said. "We need to stop these attacks before they go any further. And to do that, I need to get back to work. Dastrie, if you can find my clothes, I'll check myself out of this prison."

"Shouldn't one of the doctors examine you first, Richard?" she said.

27

"Hell, they're always poking and prodding. I feel fine other than a little stiffness, and I want to get going on this case before things get worse. So how about some help?"

"Well, I'm afraid your clothes are no longer wearable," she said. "They were covered with blood from the attack, and I had them tossed. Jeff brought you some new things an hour ago."

"Jeff?" I asked.

"Washington Jefferson," she said, smiling. "Remember? When he heard about our attack—it was featured on all the early radio programs and in the morning 'papers—he immediately came to the hospital and offered his services. I called Lizzie, and asked her to get some essentials together for Jeff to pick up. He's waiting right outside."

"Bless you both! Make sure that Lizzie gets him on the payroll immediately, with a salary triple to the one he was being paid by the city."

"Yes, boss!" she said. "Just remember that *I'm* not your secretary, Richard."

"Sorry."

Fast Eddie decided that this was a good time to make his exit, while I got dressed with the aid of my two assistants, grumping and groaning all the way—and I *really* needed their help, I was hurting so bad. But I was determined not to be a burden to anyone, and so I gritted my teeth and bulled my way through.

I may still have been a frog, but I was determined to climb out of the well and assume my rightful position again as a prince.

No mastermind of crime was going to stop The Phantom Detective. Not if I had anything to say about it!

* * * * * * *

Dastrie had a cab waiting for us at the hospital entrance. I groaned again as I sat down.

"Are you OK?" my lovely companion asked, looking at me closely. "Maybe you're getting up too soon."

"She's right, sir," Jeff said. "You really need to take it easy."

"I can't allow anyone else to be hurt," I said. "Maybe we need to get Zinc Molrad out here from our California office."

"Already on his way."

"Also, please phone my old friend, Cullen de Loos: he has fingers in many different pies, financial and otherwise. Police Sergeant Francesco Castelluccio from the Two-Two Precinct might be helpful: he's just reached retirement age, and knows the city better than most. And then there's Rubio Cocinas."

"I don't think you've ever mentioned him."

"He's an ex-con Puertoriceño from The Bronx—used to own a gym there. He still does some personal training on the side. He owes me a few favors.

"Belle Darling in Queens is another possibility: she's an old Vaudevillian. There's also a P.I. named Quentin Morlock in Brooklyn; he's another person with tentacles reaching everywhere."

"They're all in your card directory, dear?"

"If the numbers and addresses aren't current, there are other ways of locating them. Please arrange a meeting with as many of these as possible tomorrow morning at nine—including Jeff."

"You want *me* there, sir?" the black man said.

"You're either part of this team or you're not, and I'd rather have the benefit of your experience. Also, you and I need to pay a visit to Harlem this afternoon, to see if we can find any clues regarding your brother's death. You have any idea where this Ruby Diamond lives?"

"No, sir, ah don't, but the bartender might."

"Then it's a date."

By then we were back at the Brockleigh-Greeneleaffe Building, and Jeff was helping me slide out off the cab and slowly crab my way up the stone steps to the main entrance.

"Gad, I'm feeling old and worn out. I think I'll dine in," I told Jeff, "and perhaps take a nap before then, if that's all right with the both of you."

"You need your rest, Richard," Dastrie said. "Don't worry, I'll start contacting everyone."

I didn't argue with her—I just didn't have the energy. We took the elevator up to our penthouse suite, which I'd ordered remodeled into an apartment during Dastrie's convalescence in California, and gratefully headed off to bed. Even an hour or two of sleep would help revive my spirits.

But once again, the "Nasty Gnomes" returned to plague my dreams, as I was hauled before the King of the Dwarfs to receive his judgment for my trespass on his domain. Even in the midst of this unpleasant nightmare, I somehow knew that my brain was trying to send me a message. I was missing part of the big picture, and my id was pointing the way, if only I had enough sense to see it.

I strained and strained to see the little man's face, but it was always covered in shadow. Who *was* he? Why was he tormenting me?

The questions kept haunting me, until finally I came abruptly awake, covered in hot, sticky sweat.

Something was lurking down there in the darkness, just beyond my reach. I knew it would ooze out of the mud in the end. Froggie just had to be patient.

* * * * * * *

After tossing and rolling 'round and 'round for three hours, I finally slid myself out of bed, and headed for the shower, which I turned up as high as I could stand it. Then I tried to do some basic exercises, but without much success—too stiff—and asked Jeff to get me a sausage and sauerkraut roll from one of the street vendors lurking outside.

I needed something substantial to restore my depleted energy, and that foot-long dog, lathered with relish and sharp mustard and onions and mushrooms, tasted like ambrosia fit for the gods. Juices dribbled down my chin as I chomped my way through the thing and scooped up the strands of sour cabbage, and I could easily have wolfed down another. I settled instead for some steaming Darjeeling tea and a cup of pan-fried noodles and dumplings left over from our Chinese dinner several nights earlier. I washed it down with a bottle of dark ale.

Dastrie joined us a few minutes later with a glass of milk and a slice of cinnamon toast.

"Want a bite?" I said.

"No thanks," was her response—she frowned at me over her white mustache. "That can't be very good for you."

"Probably not," I agreed, "but that's not the point. It tastes wonderful, and I need to get my strength back. This is exactly what the doctor ordered!"

"Not any doctor I ever heard about."

"I like my quacks better than yours," I said.

"Quack, quack, quack," she said. It wasn't a happy "quack."

I finished the last dregs of my beer, and with Jeff's help, slowly rose to my feet.

"Where are you going?" my wife asked.

"Up the Nile to look for crocodiles—the ones who murdered Roscoe."

"You need to rest," she said. "I'm really worried about you, Richard."

"I've rested enough, *dear*!"

We stared at each other for a very long moment.

"You're serious, aren't you?" she finally said.

"I've never been more serious. I'm going out. I can't remain here while so many things are happening around us."

"Then I'm coming with you."

Jeff flagged down a cab and we headed off to Harlem. First I asked him to show me the site of his brother Roscoe's death.

The alley was located behind a nondescript building that housed a market on the first level, with several floors of apartments above.

"What was he doing here?" I asked. "Was this one of his hang-outs?"

"No, sir," Jeff said. "His body, it was found over by this bin here—but he lived way on the other side of the 'hood."

I didn't see much out of the ordinary. I tried to shift the large metal trash receptacle to see what was behind it, but in my condition I couldn't budge the thing without my companions' assistance.

"What's this?" I asked, pointing to the base of the wall. A small round opening had been punched through the bricks.

"It's them gnomes again, ain't it, sir?" Jeff asked.

"Maybe. When was Roscoe murdered? It was while we were staying in California. Around October 24th or 25th, I think. That was before the attacks began, wasn't it?"

"I read through the police reports this morning," Dastrie said. "The first mention of the gnomes was on October 31st."

"But why pick on Roscoe? What he was he doing to provoke them?"

"Ah dunno, sir. When ah asked him, he said, 'Somethin's rotten in the state of Harlem'—and he jus' laughed and laughed in that funny way of his."

"How far's the club from here?"

"Jus' a few blocks, sir. We'd best go over there now."

"I agree. There's nothing else to find here."

We'd just started pushing the trash bin back in place, when Jeff exclaimed from the other side, "What's this, sir?"

I hurried around, and together with Dastrie we pried the large can back away from the wall again. Emblazoned on the hidden side of the bin was another message written in what looked to be dried blood:

> One-Eye, are you awake?
> One-Eye, are you asleep?
> One-Eye, are you agape?

THE NASTY GNOMES, BY ROBERT REGINALD

One-Eye, are you alert?
Van Loan, are you alive?

"Roscoe's death was no accident," I said. "He was killed to make a point."

"*What* point, sir?"

"They wanted to get my attention. Well, goddam it, they have it!"

* * * * * * *

We'd deliberately left the meter running on our cab, so we'd have reliable transportation for the rest of the day. Our second stop that afternoon was The Ebonesque Club, just a few blocks from the corner of 125th Street and Lenox Avenue, in the heart of the Mount Morris District. Beneath the cold-eyed stare of the harsh winter sun, the front of the establishment looked almost naked, stripped bare of any artifice or fancy adornment. It was only when the neons lit the façade at night that the place came alive, both inside and out. Now I just saw a bum lounging in an alcove ten feet from the main entrance.

Washington Jefferson ran over and spat at the man. "Hey, you, you take youssyelf off somewheres else!" he yelled, and the wretched creature slowly staggered away, using the wall to keep himself from falling.

I was shocked.

"He's just a drunk, Jeff," I said. "Can't really help himself."

"No, sir, that he ain't," he said. "He 'jects hisself with that drug stuff to get him high. Jus' the las' few years, we have this problem down here. They call it diff'rent thin's, but it's bad juice, lemme tell you. The Puerto Ricans, they're the ones pushin' it. Make us all look bad. Anyone havin' the money, they takes thesselves somewheres else. Harlem, it ain't what it used to be, that's for goddamn sure!"

"What is?" I said, shrugging.

I looked more closely at the place where the addict had been slumped, and saw a placard that proclaimed in giant red letters:

Now Appearing!

RUBY DIAMOND

The Brown-Eyed Susan

32

Performing Her Latest Hit

THE TWO LITTLE MEN IN THE WOOD!

Assisted by those Mighty Midgets

FROGGY & TOADY

—plus a color painting of the lovely lady herself.

"Now, that's very interesting," I said. "Midgets, huh? She's quite a looker, our Miss Diamond."

"That she is, sir, though not as good as that picture makes you think," Jeff agreed. "My brother Roscoe, he come here two, three nights a week sometimes, jus' to see her. She would dance and sing and wag that little ass of hers right in front of his face—and he would laugh and say that she was the most beautifullest thing he ever did see."

"What about the midgets?" I asked.

"Well, she had this strange thin' with them, see. They were a part of the act and all. It was some kind of jazzy play. I don't rightly 'member their names, but the boss man, he would know."

As we were pushing through the doorway, I asked, "So, who's the 'boss man'?"

"A gent named Obadiah Burges, but everyone calls him Beedy, on account of those big, buggy eyes he has. He's a hard man: gotta be in this 'hood."

The interior of the club was so dark that we had to stop in our tracks to get our bearings. Finally the dim light started registering on our eyeballs.

"Can I help you?" a soft voice asked to one side.

"We're looking for the owner," I said, turning towards the man.

"I'm Mr. Burges," he said. "And you are?"

"R. C. Van Loan, of the Phantom Detective Agency, Ltd., together with my assistants, Mr. Jefferson and Miss Underhill. A man named Roscoe Wallace was murdered a few blocks from here. I'm told he used to frequent this establishment. We've been hired by his former employer's insurance company to investigate Mr. Wallace's death. His relatives are alleging that he was on company business at the time. Here's my card."

I pulled out a 3″ x 5″ paper square, only to have it snatched out of my hand.

"Maybe we'd better go to my office," came the disembodied voice, and we followed the sound of the man's footsteps back into the recesses of the building, and up a flight of stairs. He might have been leading us into Hell for all we knew.

This part of the facility was much better lit than the club itself, and I got a glimpse of Burges for the first time as he plopped behind an ornately carved ebony desk.

Jeff had been right: I was immediately drawn to the man's protruding eyeballs, which looked as if they were going to pop right out of their sockets.

"Now, who's this Wallace guy?" the owner asked.

He had no trace of an accent whatsoever, although his skin was as dark as Jeff's.

"Like I said, he worked for VL Enterprises in Manhattan. He was killed in late October behind the Mayfair Market."

"Yeah, I know the place."

"The police have no clues as to why he was murdered or who attacked him. His family is saying that he was working for his employer when he was murdered—which if true, means the insurance company has to pay ten grand to Wallace's estate. VL Enterprises has challenged the claim, saying they have no knowledge of what the man was doing there.

"We're looking into the matter for the New York State Mutual Fund. Now, I understand that Mr. Wallace's girlfriend worked here."

"Well, I have no idea," Burges said.

"Her name is Ruby Diamond. I saw her mentioned on the poster outside."

"Of course Miss Diamond works for me, but I don't know anything at all about her private life."

"What about the midgets she worked with?"

"Tiny Troubles and Wee Willie Winkie? They're OK, I guess. She was the one who insisted they be part of her act, so I had to pay her a 'little' extra on the side, if you know what I mean—and they do seem to attract a certain clientele—although Ruby herself draws better than most I've had."

"How long has she been performing here?"

Burges scratched his chin. "Oh, I don't know, three months, maybe four. I could look it up if it's important."

"Please."

He fumbled around in one of his desk drawers, pulled out a ledger, and flipped through the pages. "Oh, yeah, here it is—

September 15. I remember now: said it was her birthday. Like I said, business has been good 'cause of her. I'll be sad to see her go."

"She leaving?"

"Gave me notice a few days ago. Her last performance is New Year's Eve."

"Is Diamond her real name?"

"How the hell should I know? You really think Tiny Troubles was called that by Mommy and Daddy?" Burges said, staring at me with those godawful peepers of his. "Jeez, Van der Sloan or whatever your name is, I just sign them, I don't baby-sit them. They do the work, I pay them for their time. That's the sum total of our relationship."

"I'd really like to talk with her."

"Well, she's not here right now, OK? She works Wednesday through Sunday nights, starting at eight o'clock and closing at two the next morning. You can catch her before or after."

"But you do have an address for her, right?"

The proprietor sighed. "Yeah, course I do. Government shit and all that." He pulled out another drawer, and opened another book. "Lives in an apartment up in the Sugar Hill District." He scrawled the street and number on note paper, and then tore it off and handed it to me.

"What about the midgets?"

"Well, what about them?"

"You have addresses for them?"

"Nah, that was the thing, see: they were a package. They came with her. I paid her—she paid them. That's the way she wanted it. They were real deferential-like to her. Did everything she told them to. Ha, so do most men."

"So you don't pay Social Security for them?"

Burges cleared his throat. "Well, they're *her* employees, not mine. Wouldn't have ever hired them without her. It's *her* responsibility, Van der Sloan."

"You bet," I said. "You got anyone here who actually *knew* Ruby Diamond?"

"Dougie Manvale, the main bartender on the weekend night shift. He saw more of her than anyone else. You could talk to him. He's here now, helping to train one of our new hires. I'll call him."

The man picked up a phone, and dialed a number. "Yeah, Janie, would you send Dougie up?"

"Anything else?" he asked, making those goo-goo eyes at me again.

I shuddered. The guy gave me the willies. "No thanks. Can we use your office to interview Mr. Manvale?"

The man shrugged and got out of his chair. When Dougie knocked, Burges talked with him briefly, and then left him with us. The bartender might have been thirty-five or forty, but his face was lined, and I spotted gray streaking his temples.

I explained the situation and asked him about Ruby Diamond.

"Real purty gal," Dougie said. "Not a bad warbler, neither, although most of the puppy-dogs following her 'round could've cared less about her voice."

"You remember Roscoe Wallace?"

"Yeah, he was one of 'em, all right. Hung out here couple nights a week, at least, sniffin' in her wake. Pitiful the way they followed her."

"I take it you weren't interested."

"Seen 'em come and seem 'em go: they all look alike after a while."

"Was Ruby close to Roscoe?" Dastrie asked.

"Hmm." Dougie seemed uncomfortable with the question. "I guess so, as much as she was to anyone. She wasn't affectionate, I mean. I think she liked Roscoe, but she was always very business-like in the club. Don't know what she did outside of here. Those guys...."

"What guys?" I asked.

"I mean, they were...they were odd, that's all. The dwarfies, I'm talking about."

"*How* were they odd?"

"Well, she went through this kinda song-and-play-actin' routine with 'em—can't really describe it; it was like somethin' out of the old flicks—and she always seemed to be the one in control. At least you would think so.

"But she wasn't! Not really. If you watched 'em closely, you started noticin' thin's, like the way they corrected her.

"That's why she wasn't close to people. Whenever she got too friendly with one of the men here, one of the little guys'd sidle on over, and pipe up in his squeaky voice, 'Time to get back to work, Ruby'—and she would, every time! It was like they had this hold over her, and she couldn't fight it.

"I tried talkin' to one of the midgets once. They were in between acts, and he came over to the bar, climbed up on a stool, and asked for a drink—nothin' strong, just seltzer water—and I started askin' the usual questions about where he was from and his family

THE NASTY GNOMES, BY ROBERT REGINALD

and all. He looked me straight in the eye—gad, he was sure a cold one—and said: 'I was born with the gift of laughter, and a sense that the world was mad; and that was all my patrimony.'

"Man, didn't know what to say. You know? What *can* you say to somethin' like that? Freaked me out, it did. Then he put his glass down and went back to work."

"Mr. Burges said that it was *she* who insisted on him hiring all three of them," Dastrie said.

"Well, that may or may not have been so. But she didn't control 'em. It was the other way 'round. I seen a lot of people in this place, man, and you come so's you know folks pretty damn good—it's what you have to do to survive. You got to know when someone's had too much or is goin' to start a fight. I could see what was happenin' with my own two eyes. Hey, nothin' gets by me."

"Do you know where the midgets live?"

"Sorry, ain't got any idea. And I'm pretty sure no one else here does either. They never talked to no one, no how."

And that was the sum total of our day at The Ebonesque Club. I was tired and sore, and decided to head back to the office with Dastrie; Jeff went on home to his wife, Rosalie.

Our cab was still waiting patiently on the street. The driver made a fortune on us going nowhere that day, but that was OK. Sometimes just driving around in circles gets you further along the road than you might think.

CHAPTER FOUR

"ARE YOU LOST, DADDY?"

▲

"Are you lost, Daddy?" I asked tenderly.
"Shut up," he explained.

—Ring Lardner

▼

NEW YORK, NEW YORK
WEDNESDAY, 16 DECEMBER 1953

The first meeting of the Eastern Branch of The Phantom Detective Agency, Ltd., took place at nine the next morning in my office conference room. Other than Dastrie and myself, six others were present: Cullen de Loos, Police Sergeant Franky Castelluccio, Rubio Cocinas, Belle Darling, Quent Morlock, and "Jeff" Jefferson.

"What about Zinc Molrad?" I asked.

"His train was trapped in a blizzard east of Denver," Dastrie said. "He may be stuck there for several days."

"Why didn't he fly?"

"He doesn't like planes."

"Then we'll proceed without him." I explained that I was actually The Phantom Detective, and told them why I'd gathered them here: to establish an investigative service to handle crimes that the police couldn't resolve. "Although I've encountered each of you in the past, we have a very short time to get reacquainted.

"So if you want to become part of this new organization, I'll need a commitment from you before you leave. You're under no obligation, of course."

"I'd still want to maintain a business presence in the community," de Loos said. He was a pawn shop broker in his sixties, but also bought and sold diamonds and other precious stones.

"Of course. In fact, I would prefer that all of you maintain some of the connections or occupations that you already have, except for the good sergeant here, who would officially have to retire to avoid a conflict of interest. But if you become part of the PDA, you'd have to make yourself available to the Agency whenever and however needed, sometimes on short notice. You'd be well compensated, of course, even when you weren't actually working for us."

"What happens if I join the firm, but decide at some point that I want out?" Morlock asked.

"If you've been with us for at least a year, you'll get a severance package of six months' salary. If you're hurt on the job, I'll cover all medical expenses for as long as necessary. And if, God forbid, you're killed or permanently disabled, you or your next of kin will receive a pension for life."

"I was going to put my papers in anyway in another six months," Castelluccio said. "Count me in, Mr. Van Loan."

"Not much left for an old Vaudevillian," Belle said. "Sounds like a barrel of laughs, darling: I'm ready."

"I'm tired of bangin' 'round the ring. I say *sí*." This was Cocinas speaking.

"Ah's in it for my brother," Jeff said. "After that we'll have to see."

"The price is right," de Loos said, nodding his head.

"I'd like to think about it for a day or two," Morlock added.

"What is it with you P.I.'s anyway?" Dastrie asked. "The one we signed for our western branch turned out to be a traitor."

"So what happened to him?" the man asked.

"You might say that his employment contract was abruptly terminated." Dastrie had a wicked sense of humor.

I held up my right hand. "Like I said, folks, you're either in or you're out, but you have to decide now, Quent. I've known you for fifteen years. You have a good reputation as an investigator, no question. But we're facing a crisis here, and I don't have time to dilly-dally around. So please make up your mind."

The private dick took a deep sigh. "It's just that María wouldn't allow me to become involved in anything really dangerous. I mean, I do divorce stuff mostly, and some industrial spying: nothing violent."

"But you do know how to use a gun."

"Well, sure, you have to. I hardly ever carry one, but I have a permit."

"And how's business these days?"

Another long sigh. "Not great, I have to admit. I have good months and bad, in no particular order. I could use the regular income, no question. It's just that…all right, I'll do it! She's been after me for years to go to work for one of the larger agencies. I'll just say that's what I've done."

"And you wouldn't be telling a lie," I said. "Any other questions, folks?"

When no one replied, I continued: "Lizzie has employment papers for you to sign right after our meeting. Is that too soon for you, Franky?"

"No, I can push my retirement through by the end of the year—and I've got plenty of accumulated leave I could take before that. No, I'm fine, Mr. Van Loan."

"How many of you know how to use firearms?"

"I have the license," Rubio said. "Ees tough in the barrio."

"Well, I *don't* have a license, sweetie, but I sure as hell can shoot," Belle said. "All the world's a stage, you know."

"The rest of you will be trained on handling weapons," I said. "I want everyone to have as many capabilities as possible."

Then I outlined the nature of our problem. "What started as two different cases has now merged into one, all focused around the so-called 'Nasty Gnomes,' as the 'papers keep referring to them. But what's the real motivation here?"

"They probably want money, Mr. Van Loan," Cullen said, "that being the root of all evil."

"But if that's the case," Dastrie said, "Where's the demand letter? Other than the ambiguous messages scrawled on the alley walls, there's been nothing."

"Yeah, that's kinda strange," Franky said. "If this was a case of municipal blackmail, you'd expect to have specific terms stated up front. You know, 'Give us a million bucks or we'll blow up the subway'—or something like that. We've got nothing here other than two notes that sound almost like poems."

"*Are* they poems?" I asked, "And if so, from where? What do they mean? Why the reference to an eye? Why is my name mentioned?"

"I'll check the library," Quent said. "I've got some contacts there who might be able to help."

"I have no doubt that these attacks are intended to accomplish something, but until we can figure out the *why*, we're going to have a hard time determining the 'who'," I said.

"Well, Richard, we do know that Ruby Diamond is appearing on stage tonight with her two midgets at The Ebonesque Club," Dastrie said. "So I suggest that we might want to pay the dear lady a visit."

"Agreed," I said. "Jeff, Rubio, and Quent, I'd like you to accompany Dastrie and me. Belle, can you tell us anything about these performers?"

"Not specifically, dearie," she said. "They're a generation or two after my time. But the Little People do tend to cluster together, both in and out of the trade, and I know a few of the old-timers. Most of them are employed this time of the year as Santa's helpers."

"Elves?" Dastrie asked.

"Elves," Belle agreed. "The better establishments like to have the real thing. There's also this place called Santy's Village out on Long Island that's open all year 'round. They always have fifty or a hundred of them, even more during the Christmas season."

"Is that near Bibleland?" Quent asked.

"Oh, right down the road, sweet things. Although what Santa Claus has to do with the Bible is something I have yet to figure out, ha, ha, ha!"

"Cullen, I'd like you to put your feelers out on Wall Street, and see if you can find some underlying financial motive for the attacks—someone who might gain something from the disruption of the holiday sales season.

"Franky, I'd like you to ask around about previous midget- or dwarf-related crimes or public incidents. I would think they'd stand out from the norm."

"Will do."

At that moment, Lizzie knocked on the door to the conference room, and then popped her head inside.

"Telephone for you, Mrs. Van Loan," she said.

"Back in a moment," Dastrie said.

We were still talking about assignments when my wife rushed back into the room, her face completely drained of color.

"What's the matter?" I asked, rushing over to her.

"It's Daddy! He's disappeared! They think the gnomes have kidnapped him!"

* * * * * * *

In retrospect, I believe that this one incident was the key in cementing the relationships of our nascent organization. We had to come together very quickly, and find a means of getting along—and a crisis atmosphere always helps. It shows the strengths and weaknesses of each member of the group.

Dastrie was more than a little distracted by the threat to her father. Interestingly, it was Belle, that chunky old dame with silver hair, who picked up the pieces.

"Come on, darling," she said, putting her arm around Dastrie's shoulders, "let's go have ourselves a little cry somewhere." And then she led my lovely wife out of the room to give her a chance to compose herself.

"Franky, I'd like you to call your contacts on the force, and see what they have to say about the ex-Commissioner's disappearance."

"Right away, sir," he said, and went to find Lizzie and a private phone.

I sighed. The game was ratcheting up fast now.

Castelluccio returned ten minutes later, by which time Belle and Dastrie had rejoined us as well.

"You OK?" I asked.

"I'm fine, Richard," my wife said. "It just…it just caught me off-guard, that's all."

"What did you find out, Sergeant?" I asked.

"Doesn't look too good, sir. The Commissioner was coming out of his brownstone at eight this morning, with his driver waiting for him at the curb. As he walked down the steps, he was attacked from either side by a swarm of the gnomes. The driver pulled his gun and came to his rescue, but was killed after shooting a number of the attackers. Then they just disappeared, pulling Mr. Underhill down into the cellar with them, and from there through a large hole that had been cut through the wall into an underground passageway."

"There's no doubt it was the gnomes?"

"None. The driver lived long enough to give an account of the attack, even though he was badly beaten. He died at the hospital a little while ago."

"Well, it's almost ten now. I think we should take a break, and then meet again about one o'clock at the scene of the crime. I want to take a look underground. Dress appropriately, folks.

"Belle and Cullen, I know you're physically unable to handle this kind of exercise, so Belle, I'd like you to take this opportunity to find out what you can about the midget community, and Cullen, to investigate a potential financial motive for the crime. Franky, you better get back to the Two-Two.

"Quent, see if you can find information on possible ways of getting into the underground tunnels in that area. With the former Commissioner kidnapped, we've just lost our official police access—which may be why he was removed from the investigation. Franky can only do so much out of the Two-Two Precinct without raising red flags. Rubio, I want you to select some weapons from my locker to use in the underground. Jeff, you can work with Lizzie to help establish a communications command post here.

"OK? I'll see all of you at one."

* * * * * * *

Dastrie was too upset to eat lunch, so I just held her close for a while, and then suggested we take a nap. I still hadn't regained my stamina; bruises were livid on my legs, buttocks, and torso. Finally I managed to drift off into a dreamless sleep.

At eleven-thirty my lovely companion nudged me awake. I took a quick shower, munched on a tuna sandwich, and then pulled a few weapons from my hidden gun closet in back of the *real* closet.

"I'll stick with my own, thanks," she said, when I tried handing her a Luger. "I'm more comfortable with it."

I also pulled out some torches for ourselves, Rubio, and Quent.

Franky called a few minutes later. "Something's come up at the station," he said, "and I can't get away right now. However, you want to look at Tunnel 214. That's where the trail ran out. Be watchful: I think the detectives are all gone now, but you never know."

"Don't worry about us. We'll be fine," I said.

I phoned Quent with the news, and when he told me he'd found a way to get into the underground, I asked him to bring along a set of lock picks and a crowbar.

Dastrie and I took a cab to her old neighborhood near Central Park, and exited about a block away from the Underhill home. There we rendezvoused with the other three members of our spelunking team.

"Over here," Quent said, leading us into another alley. He pointed to a small metal door near the back of one building: "This may take a few minutes."

But he actually forced the lock in about thirty seconds. "Cheap city crap," he muttered under his breath, as he creaked the aperture open. Inside was an iron ladder leading into the depths, lit by a single pale bulb.

I took the lead, slowly feeling my way down into the damp dark, flashing the torch around with each creaky step. The others followed in order, one at a time.

It was about twenty feet to the bottom. There was another small metal door (unlocked) on the side of the square terminal room. I carefully pushed it open, and peered out into the tunnel. Bare bulbs provided a faint illumination every ten feet or so. I saw no one in either direction.

"It's OK," I whispered, stepping out of the opening. The others were right behind me.

Tunnel 214 had once been part of the underground subway system that burrowed beneath the city and its suburbs. The rusted tracks were still there, waiting for a train that would never come again.

"What ees thees place?" Rubio asked.

"When they rebuilt the lines—several times actually—they cut off several tunnels and drilled new ones to reconfigure the layout, supposedly to make the trains operate more efficiently," Quent said. "Some of the older sections were just abandoned, and this was obviously one of them."

"Ees very strange."

"Look over here!" Dastrie said.

We hurried to where she was examining a section of the roadbed with her flashlight. In between the obscuring footprints of the police and city workers, we could see the imprint of what looked like a child's foot.

"The gnomes?" I asked.

"I think so," she said.

She carefully followed the trail until we came to another metal door on the opposite side of the tunnel, a hundred feet further on.

"They went in here."

It was another exit into Hell. Whatever lights might have existed at one time had either burnt out or been deliberately destroyed. We shined our torches down into the depths, and could see nothing.

"Here we go again," I said, stepping onto the first rung of the ladder.

And down and down and down we went. The old railway tunnel had been cool and dry. This new place, whatever it was, was warm and wet.

Finally the ladder went through the ceiling of an open room and down one brick wall. When I heard something sloshing, I flashed my lamp below. I could see the sheen of running water, and smell the stench of raw sewage.

"Ah, the Cloacus Maximus," I said, stepping down onto the mossy green stone.

"Jeez," Quent hissed, as he plopped down beside me in the muck. "That's pretty foul."

The run-off was only a few inches deep at its worst—just enough to fill our shoes with the stuff—but the stench was overpowering.

"Gad," Dastrie said. "This is awful."

"That's not the worst part," I said. "The trail ends here, folks. There's no way to know for sure which way they went through this crap."

"They probably went uptown," she said. "All the previous incidents took place between here and Harlem."

"Ah thinks so too," Jeff said.

"We don't know that for a fact," I said, "but I'm willing to pursue this further, if you are. We could either split into two teams, one going in each direction, or stay together."

"If we actually encounter the gnomes, we're going to need everyone we've got," Quent said. "There's too many of them to fight with two or three people."

They all nodded their heads in agreement.

"Very well, then, that's what we'll do." And so we started upstream towards Harlem.

The going was very slow. The tunnel was old and slippery, the footing treacherous. Jeff fell in once, but jumped up right away and went on, brushing himself off. His determination was a beacon for us all. We found no traces of anyone having passed this way, other than an occasional scrape on a mossy wall—but these could have been made at any time in recent history.

Every hundred feet or so a smaller (sometimes much smaller) side tunnel or pipe would intersect with ours; most of these were impassable due to their narrow apertures. The current was against us, but the flow was relatively shallow and mild. We hadn't had a significant rainstorm in Manhattan in several weeks.

We'd walked almost forty-five minutes before it happened. Suddenly I heard a splash up ahead, just the other side of a bend in the tunnel, and I flashed my torch forward. At first I could see nothing, but then I noticed the myriad pinpricks of light reflected back at me—and when one of them blinked, I realized what was happening.

"Go back!" I yelled at the others.

No one needed any prompting. We turned and began running down that interminable tube of death.

THE NASTY GNOMES, BY ROBERT REGINALD

It was the damndest flight I'd ever been involved with—completely silent save for the gasping of our breaths and the splashing of our feet. But despite our much longer strides, the little buggers somehow managed to stay with us.

"Gotta stop!" Jeff exclaimed, heaving out loud. He was more out of shape than the rest of us.

He abruptly halted, leaning against the side of the tunnel, taking huge, wheezing breaths of the foul air.

"Stop!" I ordered the gnomes—and astonishingly they did, just out of range of my light.

The four of us who were armed drew our weapons and formed a defensive line. For a moment, nothing happened.

Finally, I heard a faint, squeaky voice emanating from out of the dark, somewhere from behind the enemy's line:

"S-so, Mis-ter Van Loan, you would kill us-s without reas-son."

"Where have you taken Commissioner Underhill?" I asked.

"To the North Pole, where he will be s-safe."

"And is the North Pole close by?"

"As-s clos-se as-s you wish-sh it to be," came the reply.

"Who *are* you?"

"One-Eye, King of the Gnomes-s."

"What do you want?"

"We want what you want: lif-fe, liberty, and the purs-suit of happiness-s."

"Sorry, Your Majesty, there has to be a reckoning for your crimes."

"Our crimes-s, oh yes-s. There has-s to be a reckoning for *your* crimes-s, Mis-ter Van Loan, your crimes-s."

"I repeat: *what do you want?*"

"A million dollars-s for the releas-se of the Underhill."

"Money, again. It always comes down to the money in the end." I spat into the sewer of life.

"Thos-se who have everything think money is-s nothing. Thos-se who have nothing think money is-s everything."

I sighed. "Very well: when and where do you want the drop made?"

"That mes-sage is waiting for you to find. But we want more."

"More?"

"Yes-s. We als-so want *you*, Mis-ter Van Loan. We will give you the Underhill alive, but you will take his-s plac-ce with us-s."

"Agreed."

"No, Richard!" Dastrie said. "No, you can't do that. You...."

46

"Agreed," I repeated, ending the discussion. There was something else going on here, and the game could only end one way.

But there was no reply, and the lights twinkling in the firmament of the Cloacus Maximus of the City of New York suddenly blinked out.

The Nasty Gnomes were gone!

* * * * * * *

But they had lied: there was nothing waiting for us back at the office—no message, no ransom demand, no instructions.

"Damn them anyway!" I yelled, banging my hand on the desk and then shaking it in pain.

Suddenly I realized Dastrie was crying again. It was her father we were talking about, after all. I folded her into my arms and held her close.

"What do you want us to do, boss?" Quent asked.

I broke the embrace and turned around.

"You did very well today, all of you, but we're not through yet. We still have our rendezvous at The Ebonesque Club. Meet us there at seven-thirty. Then we'll see what this Miss Diamond knows—not to mention Froggy and Toady!"

After they left, we cleaned up, and I had Lizzie order us some egg rolls and sizzling scallops and Szechuan bean sprouts from the Zhang-Grill-Ah! Emporium, and we retired to our quarters, where Dastrie and I picked over the light but tasty dinner. Neither of us had much of an appetite, but we still had to bolster our energy for the night's work yet to come.

"I just don't understand, Richard," she said. "Why did they kidnap my father?"

"I think they wanted leverage, and thought this was the best way to get it."

"But a police official, even a retired one? Cops will protect their own, always. No matter what happens to Daddy, they'll never stop looking for the gnomes and their 'King'—and they're liable to shoot first and ask questions later. They'll make an example out of them."

"So would I," I said. "This kind of rampant disregard for public safety can't be allowed to continue. It encourages others to follow suit."

"We're beginning to sound like old fogies," she said, sighing. "It's different when it's someone else's pain, isn't it? But when it's

47

your pain, you just want it over—and your family back again in one piece."

"Yes, I think that's true."

"You never talk much about your family, Richard."

"Not much to say, really: they're all dead."

"But who were they?"

I didn't really want to discuss this now, but I could see that I had no choice: if not now, then later, and meanwhile the topic would continue to fester just beneath the surface of our relationship.

"You know that I served as a pilot during the Great War," I said.

She nodded, so I continued.

"In mid-September 1918, with the Bosch everywhere in retreat, I received a wire from my father. My sister June, my only sibling, had disappeared. She was a year younger than me, a sweet-natured, beautiful girl with great prospects. She'd just vanished.

"Of course, I couldn't possibly get permission to return home: they needed every experienced man they had at the front. Two days later, I got the bad news: June's body had been found, raped and mutilated, in the basement of our family estate. My father was accused of the crime.

"Before the war ended in November—and I was finally allowed to leave for home—Dad had been tried and convicted; he was executed the day after I returned. He swore to me in our final interview that he'd had nothing to do with June's murder—and I believed him. Within months, my mother suffered a nervous breakdown, and then had to be committed to a mental institution.

"I had to sell the estate to pay our legal and medical bills. Dad's partner, Peter Maussey, bought out our share of the business, but at a severely discounted price. He produced papers that he said showed mismanagement and poor planning by my father, and stated that he was doing us a favor paying *anything* for the firm, since it was nearly bankrupt.

"I salvaged enough cash to pay for Mom's treatment and to get a college education, but not at one of the posh ivy-league schools for which I'd been intended. I went to a Jesuit college instead, and there I learned how to reason and how to plot and how to act.

"When I graduated, I used my new-found skills in logic and analysis to investigate our old firm, and discovered that it had been sound all along—Maussey had paid far less for Dad's majority share than was fair or just.

"I confronted the man, and he just laughed at me. I told him what a cad he was, and he said: 'You Van Loans always think you're better than everyone else. Your sister was like that too. When I asked her to marry me, the bitch told me I wasn't nearly good enough for her. I went to see Curtis to ask his help, but he told me he would never give his permission for the union. When I talked to Marjorie, she said her daughter would only marry for love, not money, and June would have the final say in the matter.

"'Well, the shoe's on the other foot now, isn't it? It's all gone to shit, hasn't it, Little Richie? No house, no business, no family. I hope your *dear* mother rots away in that cell of hers in the asylum. And as for you, my boy, you can go straight to Hell'."

"My God!" Dastrie said. "What kind of man would say such things?"

"It gets worse.

"I was suspicious enough to investigate Maussey's background, and discovered a history—carefully papered over, of course—of sexual assaults and batteries on women. In another state, under another name, he'd been accused of murdering a young girl, but had gotten off on a technicality. He'd beaten his first wife almost to death. But there was nothing in the way of physical evidence to link him to my sister's crime, and I knew if I accused him of June's murder, he would slip the noose once again.

"So I watched him quietly for over a year, until he finally made a business trip to the big city to attend a convention. He went looking for a prostitute one night north of Central Park, and he found me instead. I wore a mask. I carried two guns—and I finally found a measure of justice, a purpose in life. The police called it a routine mugging, and no one much lamented Maussey's untimely passing.

"Over the next few years, I gradually became The Phantom, with Frank Haven's help. But that's another story."

"Did this Peter leave any family?"

"He'd remarried again—his third or fourth wife by this time—after taking over Dad's business, using his new-found wealth to secure himself a society spouse. I never met her, but I believe she inherited all of his—all of *our*—estate. They had several children, I think, and I know he also had kids by one of his earlier wives, although my folks would never discuss them for some reason. The business was bought out by some conglomerate after his death—and then went bankrupt during the Depression."

"That's one of the saddest stories I've ever heard. No wonder you don't like talking about them."

I went over to the dresser, and pulled out a grainy photograph showing our family as it was in 1917, with me towering in the background.

"I've seen this before," she said. "They look like nice folks."

"They were genuinely *good* people," I said. "And I miss them every day that I live. Avenging their deaths was easy, but it started me down a road that I've often regretted. There never seems to be any end to the filth that I have to clean up. Am I God's avenger, or just another criminal with better self-justifications? I don't know."

"You're a good man, Richard," Dastrie said.

"Perhaps, but I never think of myself in such terms. However, we're wasting time—now we need to move on."

* * * * * * *

At night The Ebonesque Club was a fairy wonderland of light and sight and sound and action. As each car rolled up to the main entrance, a valet would hand the passengers out the doors, and give the driver a small paper ticket. Privately owned vehicles were then shepherded away to a monitored lot nearby.

We could hear the jazz band blaring through the open doors as our cab stopped at the curb. Dastrie wore a long, sweeping dress in green silk, and I marveled again at her beauty and poise as I gave her my right arm. I felt her tremble beside me: the stress of worrying about her father was getting to her, but she had insisted on accompanying me.

The others of our little group were already waiting for us inside.

Within the club proper, the music was so loud that we could barely talk without shouting. Al's Jazzier Rah was the name of the combo, and they made up in noise for any absence of talent. Actually, the drummer, Ring-O somebody-or-other, was quite good. But I never cared much for all the sax and brass, and that's what the rest of them played.

"Great stuff!" Jeff said, grinning from ear to ear. To each his own!

We had to order drinks at inflated prices to remain at the table near the stage, but I had them go heavy on the seltzer—all of us needed clear heads tonight.

Promptly at eight o'clock, the interminable racket finally ceased—just for a moment—and Burges appeared front and center.

"And now, ladies and gents, the moment you've all been waiting for!" he announced in that solemn voice of his. "I give you the golden-tongued warbler herself—Rrrruuubbbyyy Dddiammmond!"

There was a pause, and just for a moment, I wondered if the singer was actually going to appear. Bug-eyed Beedy glanced around nervously when she didn't immediately step onto the stage.

But then there she was, wrapped in a kind of feather cloak that covered her entire body except her face. The enthusiasm of the applause surprised me. It was obvious that Ruby engendered numerous repeat customers.

At first I didn't see anything remarkable about the woman, but when she started to sing—and slowly peal back the covering—I had to gulp. She had a body that Troy, New York would have launched their ships for, round and firm and glowing with need. She was lighter in color than I expected—or perhaps it was just the way the spots lingered over her mostly revealed charms—but the cumulative effect of her sexy attitude and perfectly proportioned limbs was overpowering. It yelled "Come hither!" to every male in the room.

And when she opened wide her mouth and filled the area with that lovely sound, I discovered what "warbling" really meant. The jazz musicians provided a muted accompaniment in the background, and I realized that they knew how to play other instruments beside the saxophone.

But that voice! Oh, man!

It was every boy's wet dream, every man's lost love, every codger's last lament. It ranged up and down the scale, singing of—I know not what—and it beckoned and pleaded, and it pushed and it prodded, and it spoke of love and lust and loss. I could have listened to that woman for the rest of my days, and never tired of her song.

And then the midgets appeared, one to either side, and the music began running up the scale into peril and tragedy and lament. She uttered words—but to this day, I couldn't tell you exactly what she said. And those two little men, they danced and pranced all around her, hailing her as a goddess among women.

For two hours I watched, wholly unaware of the passage of time. And then she stopped and bowed, and her two sidekicks bowed along with her, and they all left the stage.

A great sigh filled the room as every man in the place suddenly released his breath.

"Well, I certainly don't understand what Roscoe saw in her," Dastrie said. Then she looked at each of us in turn. "What?"

"Oh, she was wonderful!" Quent said.

"*¡Como la canaria bella!*" Rubio added.

"*Now* I understand what my brother saw!" Jeff said.

"Understand *what*?" Dastrie asked. "What's the matter with you all?"

"Tell us what *you* saw," I said.

"Well, she's comely, no question about that, but not spectacularly so. She can carry a tune, but her singing's nothing to write home about. And those two little guys, why, they're just grotesque. I mean, I don't know why she even bothers to have them there. They add nothing to her act."

"The men in this place," I said, trying to explain in simple terms to my dear wife, "Were absolutely mesmerized by her performance. All of them."

"Really?" She looked at each of us in turn. "Truly? How very strange. I didn't get that at all. I just don't see her appeal."

Then Ruby emerged on stage again, and all eyes, all *male* eyes, immediately refocused on her. But she wasn't there to perform. Instead, she waltzed down the wooden step, sashaying from side to side with those big round hips of hers, and sauntered over to one of the tables to our right and spoke with the two men sitting there. I could see them laughing together, and I was jealous of the privilege.

She repeated this with each of the groups in the first couple of rows, until she finally, lamentably late in the game, discovered us!

"You're new here, aren't you?" she hissed—and I loved her for asking the question!

"Ah, y-yes, this is our f-first time," I said, stammering like a school boy. Her perfume—rich and oily and cloying and spicy—just about knocked me over. What the bloody hell was the matter with me?

"Well, I certainly do hope it won't be your last."

"N-no, ah, n-no! Of course n-not."

"Would you sign my napkin?" Quent said, looking very much like a puppy-dog waiting for a treat.

She took his proffered fountain pen, lazily unscrewed it, and then very carefully wrote, "Love, Ruby," in large rounded letters. She handed him back his pen, and pressed the cloth to her lips, leaving an impression in ruddy red gloss just beneath her signature.

"I sure hope that will do," she said.

I thought Quent was going to faint dead away.

"Oh, *pul-ease!*" Dastrie muttered, just loud enough for me to hear—but someone else heard her too.

Ruby abruptly swiveled her lovely head around like a praying mantis, piercing my wife with her harsh black eyes.

"I'm sorry if I can't 'pul-ease' everyone," the performer said—and then, suddenly, I could see her turn "it" on, whatever *that* was, and deliberately try to seduce my female companion!

Dastrie just frowned back at her. She wasn't in a mood to play games, not with her father kidnapped. "I'm not buying any of it, sister," she said, "so take your wares somewhere else. You can't have *him* either." She touched her hand to my shoulder.

"Well, I guess not," Ruby said. Then she turned her lovely back on us and walked away, retreating into her dark den behind the stage.

We waited until her second performance at 10:30, which was pretty much a repeat of the first, although some of the music was subtly altered. Now that I'd regained control of my senses, I paid somewhat more attention to the "tricks of the trade," so to speak, and watched Miss Diamond's antics very carefully. The magic, it seemed, emanated not only from her voice, but curiously, also from the movements of her two miniature assistants.

They were a bit larger than normal for midgets, and their heavily made-up facial features were deliberately grotesque. The playlet itself seemed to focus on the underworld of German mythology, in which the dwarfs were following their mighty king into glorious battle against the demon forces of the dark goddess. The verses were sung in an archaic form of the old high language, much of which I didn't understand. My college German simply wasn't up to the task.

The third, somewhat shorter rendition began at 12:30 and lasted until two. We were waiting at the stage door for Ruby to appear when the last strains of music faded away.

We were still there at three.

"I'm freezing, Richard, and I'm awfully tired," Dastrie said. "Maybe we ought to go home."

We went around to the front door of the club, which was locked, of course, and pounded on it until one of the cleaning crew emerged from her hole.

"We want to see Miss Diamond," I said.

"All gone," the woman said, waving her arm in the air. "No one left here now."

"Crap!" I said. "She must have departed through the front."

So we gave the bad news to our comrades-in-arms, and then all headed home. It had been a long and sad day, and we had not got on in the world very well at all. Yes, we knew more than we had previously, but as to what it meant....

I arranged the next meeting of The Phantom Detective Agency for nine in the morning. Dastrie checked in with her mother, and then we went off to bed.

CHAPTER FIVE

THE POLICEMAN'S LOT

▲

When constabulary duty's to be done,
The policeman's lot is not a happy one.
—Gilbert & Sullivan

▼

NEW YORK, NEW YORK
THURSDAY, 17 DECEMBER 1953

The next morning dawned cold and sleety, with a layer of ice making the streets and buildings a frigid fantasyland. Nonetheless, all the members of our new Agency managed to stagger into the office by ten o'clock, and I had donuts and bagels and hot coffee and chocolate waiting in the conference room to help take away the chill. Also present was Zinc Molrad, who thought the bad weather had followed him all the way from Denver.

"Man, it's foul out there!" Franky Castelluccio said, as he removed his scarf, stomped his feet, and unzipped his coat. "It's supposed to snow later. They say we could have blizzard-like conditions by the weekend."

"Well, that should certainly help with the pest control," Quent said.

"I hope so. Our boys are putting in a lot of overtime, but we haven't had much luck in catching the little buggers."

Everyone had settled down now, and were munching or sipping or even cogitating. I brought Belle and Franky and Cullen up-to-date with the previous day's developments, and then asked the police sergeant to comment.

"Yes sir, you wanted me to look for previous incidents involving dwarfs as either criminals or victims," Franky said.

"I think they prefer to be called 'Little People'," Belle said.

55

"Yeah, whatever," he said. "At any rate, there wasn't much, and a lot of that was anecdotal. I did talk with some of the older members of the force. Most of what I found was minor graft or thievery, some of it related to circus or carnival shows. Nothing that really stands out.

"But I did hear a story that sparked my interest. About five years ago, a twenty-eight-year-old actor called Petite Souris—he was one of the Munchkins in *The Wizard of Oz*—was supposedly mugged and raped by a gang in Central Park, and nearly died from his wounds. He would never say who attacked him—claimed he didn't remember anything at all about the incident. But after he recovered, maybe a year later, the bodies of several young toughs suddenly began sprouting up all over the city—more than the usual number, you understand—and all of them mutilated in the same way, with their private parts cut off and stuffed in their mouths. Five corpses were recovered in all. Some of our guys think that Souris had a hand in the murders. He was questioned but never charged. We had no evidence directly linking him with the crimes."

"Could the killings have been routine gangland retribution?" Dastrie asked.

"Sure," Franky said. "It happens."

"So what became of this little actor?" de Loos asked.

"He disappeared from the police records in 1950, and no one on the force seems to know anything else about him."

"A man like that just doesn't vanish," the pawn shop owner said. "He would have left traces of some sort. Maybe I can locate him through my own sources."

"Please follow up and let us know," I said. "In the meantime, what else have you found, Cullen?"

"There're all kinds of ways that a man can profit from bad times," he said, "*If*, that is, one knows they're coming. A poor Christmas season could push stock prices down, affect certain futures, depress the value of the big department stores, and so forth, depending on how long the catastrophe lasted and how much sales were off. But you could make thousands, even millions, if you knew what you were doing and had the capital to do it with."

"And if the City of New York ransoms ex-Commissioner Underhill, they might have that capital," I said.

"Surely they wouldn't do that, Richard," my wife said.

"I hope not. Belle, what can you tell us about the local community of Little Folks?"

"Well, dearie, there seem to be a great many of them in the metropolitan area," she said. "They come here for both work and companionship. There's a community center in Harlem owned by a group called the Fraternal Rotary of Gnomes, which provides assistance to the Little People, helping them get jobs and whatever else they need. No one seems to know where the money comes from to support this organization. This agency also has an office in Santy's Village out near Ronkonkoma on Long Island. A lot of the wee folk are employed there year 'round; in fact, there's a rumor that the Rotary actually owns the park, although the Village managers are all normal-sized people. I've performed there once or twice myself. It's a very strange place: the employees wear badges with the image of a unicycle surrounding a number."

"How odd," Dastrie said. "Are the numbers all different?"

"I do believe so, sweetie."

Lizzie popped her head in: "Sergeant, you have a phone call."

"Sorry, Mr. Van Loan," he said, "I had to give them your number here. I can't take much time off with what's going on in the city."

"It's all right," I said.

We could hear him through the open door as he spoke into the receiver: "Castelluccio here, from the Two-Two. Yeah, *really*? Where do I report? Yes, sir, I'll be right there."

"What's up?" I asked, when he returned.

"The City's received a ransom demand for Commissioner Underhill. They've apparently agreed to pay...."

"What!" we all shouted simultaneously.

Dastrie turned white and looked as if she was going to faint. "Thank God," she exclaimed.

"...And the exchange is supposed to take place this afternoon."

"Where?" I asked.

"The kidnappers haven't said yet, or named the exact hour of the drop. They're going to phone this in later, so we won't have much time to set up. But we'll do it anyway, of course. We're finally going to catch the leaders of the Nasty Gnomes!"

I hoped he was right, but I suspected the task would be more difficult than that, judging by our previous experience.

"Let me know what you hear, if you can do so without jeopardizing your position." I said. "In the meantime, I'll call around, and see if we can be an official part of this exercise."

But when I reached Assistant Chief Jacob Wilhelm, Underhill's second-in-command on the task force, he refused even to consider our participation.

"I know Mr. Underhill thought very highly of you and your agency, Mr. Van Loan," he said, "but we have a procedure to follow here."

"But I thought those procedures included never negotiating with kidnappers."

"This is a special case, sir, and the Mayor has decided that Mr. Underhill's life is more important than any specific departmental policy. We'll be very careful about making the exchange: no Commissioner, no money."

"But why not include us as backup?"

"We're going to have dozens, if not hundreds, of official police and security forces on site. You'll just get in the way. I'm sorry, Mr. Van Loan, but even the time and place of the meeting are highly confidential. You can read about it in the newspapers—and Mr. Underhill will be happy to brief you, I'm quite sure, when he's released."

"Thank you," I said, hanging up the line. I nodded at Lizzie to cut off the speaker. "All right, folks, you heard what he said."

"So what time do you want us there, boss?" Zinc said, arching his eyebrows.

I just laughed.

"Yes, we'll be there, folks, one way or the other, even if we don't hear anything from Franky."

As much as possible, I wanted to preserve Castelluccio's access to official sources even after he retired, so I didn't want him to compromise himself now.

"Quent, you and Zinc monitor the official Police broadcasts. We've got a room on the fourth floor with all of the latest radio equipment. We'll soon find out the where and when of this exercise. And then we'll all join the tea party, at least in the background."

* * * * * * *

Franky never called, as I half expected, so we listened and waited, taking turns, pair by pair, at the radio set upstairs.

Finally Rubio came running into the conference room; Belle remained behind to monitor the official channels.

"*Señor*," he almost shouted, "we have it!"

The rendezvous was to take place at five o'clock at the entrance to a beat-up apartment building off Amsterdam Avenue in the Sugar Hill district of Harlem.

"Ah knows that place, sir," Jeff said. "It's a bad street, with lots of dirty alleys and hidin' spots. The buildings, they're all gettin' run-down and full of them rats, both two-legged and four-legged. Not somewheres you wants to be after dark."

And at this time of the year in the Big Apple, sunset was closer to four P.M. than five.

Morlock was already pulling out detailed maps of the neighborhood, including one that displayed all the buildings there.

"The Police will set up here, here, and here," Quent said, pointing to the obvious posts and road blocks. "They'll have several layers of security in place, so if one fails, another'll pick up the slack."

"What about underground?" I asked.

"There aren't any complete diagrams of the hollows beneath the city," he said. "I'm sure they'll send some teams to the obvious tunnels and conduits, but I don't see how they'll be able to find them all."

"I don't want us down there either. The gnomes have a distinct advantage in those areas. No, let's find a site far enough away that we won't be bothered by any official presence, but still can observe from the roof-top what happens down below. I want a mobile radio set with us as well, so we can continue monitoring the official channels.

"It's nearly noon. Let's order in some lunch, and then get our equipment organized, while continuing to monitor the police network. I want to move out by three. Be prepared for a frigid environment. It won't be fun out there."

My words proved an understatement. I had our team ferried in three cabs, and everything went fine until we reached our destination in Harlem. The old office building that we wanted to use was pad-locked.

"I wonder how long thees place has been abandoned," Rubio said.

"Not long, I think," I said. "It would have been vandalized otherwise."

We went around back and broke through the rear door with a crowbar. We used torches to light our way up the darkened stairs, until we reached the exit to the roof—also locked—which we also forced.

Up above we had no protection from the elements. The light breeze and dank mist made the twenty-five-degree temperature seem much colder. We set up our station on the side nearest the projected drop point—and then just watched and waited, using binoculars and a small telescope to keep an eagle eye on the proceedings. The street lights cast enough of a glow for us to see the main entrance of the apartment complex, a set of six railed stairs that climbed up to the porch and doorway.

"Damn, it's freezing up here," Quent said, knocking his gloved hands together. I could see his breath.

"And getting chillier by the minute," Dastrie added, sipping on some hot coffee out of a thermos. Her face was grim with worry.

Promptly at five the drama began. We could hear the intermittent exchanges blurting over the official channels.

Only one of the high-ranking police brass had been allowed to approach the final half-block leading up to the old structure. We saw him waiting just off the curb on the opposite side of the street from the apartment. Then the door to the building opened, and six of the gnomes brought out a stretcher with a carefully wrapped body tied to it. I was amazed: they shouldn't have been able to tote such a heavy burden, but seemed to have no trouble doing so. They slowly descended the steps, and stopped when they reached the street. Then they carefully laid down the body on the sidewalk.

"He's moving forward to make the exchange," bleeped the com.

We saw the official cautiously cross the street and approach the stretcher. He was dragging a heavy sack behind him. Five of the gnomes withdrew up the steps, pulling out their revolvers and stopping on the landing; one remained behind at the front of the mobile bed. The cop pointed to the shroud covering the head of the recumbent figure, and the little man pulled back the blanket just enough to reveal the captive's face, and also note the captive's breath misting the frigid air. Then the creature restored the cover and held out his empty hands; his comrades continued aiming their weapons at the hostage.

The official tossed the bag to the lone gnome, who again had no trouble handling the large mass of hundred- and thousand-dollar bills; he quickly checked inside the container, and then slung the sack backwards to his companions, who immediately threw it through the doorway. In an instant they were all gone, leaving the stretcher parked on the sidewalk.

Cops poured into the street and grabbed the bundle, carrying its precious cargo to safety.

As soon as they were clear, the radio came alive again: "We've got him!" it screeched. "He's alive!"

"Oh, thank God!" Dastrie exclaimed. "I've got to go down there, Richard."

"Wait!" I said, grabbing her arm. "I don't trust any of them."

Another bleat of the official radio channel: "All forces, redeploy"—I saw armed officers moving into strategic positions around the main entrance to the place.

"Look!" I said to Dastrie.

"What are they doing?" she asked.

"All men, attack!" the com shouted. "Take the building! Take the building!"

Hordes of policemen immediately swarmed into the structure front and back, and soon we could hear the distant rat-a-tat-tat of shots being exchanged in rapid order.

"Officer down!" the com screamed. "Officer down! We need an ambulance!"

"Goddam, they're everywhere!" a second person said. "Why, They're...."—but that particular channel abruptly went dead.

"What's happening?" a third voice said.

Then smoke began streaming from the windows of the upper floors.

"We have a fire!"

"We need medics!"

"We have multiple severe trauma injuries!"

"Officers down!"

"Two confirmed dead, no, three, no, four!"

"Send help now!"

And so it went, on and on and on, this developing disaster in public and private policy. I was glad now that we'd shared no part of the operation. We continued to observe from a distance as the apartment complex burned to the ground. I couldn't let Dastrie go to her father yet—it was just too dangerous out on the streets.

"He needs me," she said over and over again, pleading her case.

"We'll go together as soon as it's safe," I assured her.

But we had to wait six long and very cold hours before the operation down below subsided sufficiently to allow us to vacate the area.

We finally shut down our observation post at eleven, and each of us crept back to his or her home, discouraged and disheartened by what we'd seen. Once again we'd been fooled and foiled by old

King One-Eye and his merry men—and what was his, still remained his.

Fifteen officers had been killed by the gnomes, and fourteen others were missing and presumed dead in the fire and subsequent collapse of the structure—not to mention five firemen and a captain. The number of civilian casualties was unknown, but continued to rise as the night progressed. No intact bodies of the gnomes were recovered, just pieces. Forty-five other officers suffered injuries of various kinds. The police did not locate the million dollars in ransom money.

But the one good thing that remained of all these shenanigans was the recovery of Dastrie's father—beaten and bruised and partially starved, to be sure—but alive and safe and well on the road to renewed health. We visited him at midnight at Memorial Hospital.

"Thanks," was all he was able to gasp out, while Dastrie and mother Zenobia each held tightly to one of his hands.

A simple "Thanks" was quite enough for my wife, however. I had the good sense to say nothing, but just sat there quietly by her side. I left her there to be with her family in their time of need, and went on home.

CHAPTER SIX

TUNNELING
▲

We don't see the end of the tunnel, but I must say,
I don't think it is darker than it was a year ago,
and in some ways lighter.
—John F. Kennedy
▼

NEW YORK, NEW YORK
FRIDAY, 18 DECEMBER 1953

Early that morning, I donned my dark veneer once again, and headed back to the site of the shoot-out with the Nasty Gnomes. When I arrived, however, fire- and policemen were scurrying around everywhere, and I couldn't approach the place any closer than before.

I didn't know what I was looking for specifically, but the rage that fired the red-hot coals deep within my soul kept me searching for anything that I could tie to the case. Ruby Diamond was still a loose end, so I turned next to the address in the Sugar Hill District where she supposedly lived. I got there about the time her act was ending at The Ebonesque Club; I found myself a lonely alcove, and waited for her to appear.

Sure enough, about 2:30 a cab creaked to a halt outside the front stoop, and Ruby emerged with one of the Little People. She leaned over to hug him, spoke a couple of words, and then bounded up the steps while he got back into the vehicle.

I remained outside for another thirty minutes, until the lights went out in her apartment, and the street became as quiet as a mausoleum. I was patient, oh yes, and when I emerged from the patch of blackness that shadowed my figure, I slid up to the landing, and hid myself in the cave of the entranceway.

I always carried a small set of skeleton keys with me on my rangings through the urban wasteland, and I very patiently and silently worked at the lock until I felt it give underneath my ministrations. This allowed me access to the main lobby.

The building had originally been a rich man's mansion, but at some point had been subdivided into apartments. I knew the location of Ruby's rooms from the light she'd flicked on and off just a few minutes earlier. By now, I knew, she'd be safely tucked away in Slumberland.

I carefully picked the lock of her apartment door, and slowly pushed it open. Once inside, I waited until my sight adjusted. My night vision was enhanced through the regular ingestion of certain drugs that I imported from the Far East, and once I allowed my eyesight to adjust, I could see almost as well in the dark as I could in twilight—enough to navigate my way through a wreckage of old furniture.

The entrance to her bedroom was wide open. I could hear her regular breathing emanating from inside. I infiltrated the dark and tiptoed softly inside, one careful step at a time, until I was standing right next to the top of the bed. Then I reached down and grabbed her by the throat with my gloved right hand, pinning her head to the pillow like a bug impaled on a pin.

"Umph!" was all she could utter, as she surged awake beneath me, wiggling wildly to get loose.

"Quiet!" I whispered. "If you struggle, lady, I'll squeeze the damned life out of you!"

Still, she thrashed around like a fish being played on a line, trying to pry the iron bar of my muscled arm away from her neck. I tightened my vise and she suddenly went limp.

When she came to again, she could still feel the now-lightened caress of my hard fingers strumming on her voice box.

"I have your life within the grip of my hand," I hissed in her ear. "Be careful, dearie, lest you waste it for nothing."

"Wh-who are you? Wh-what do you w-want?" she managed to gasp out.

I had her now!

"Information. I want…information."

"You won't get it."

"By hook or by crook—I will!"

I squeezed her lovely smooth throat like a tube of tired toothpaste, pulling the life out of her. I could feel the power coursing through my body, and I wanted to end it right then and there. It was all I could do to keep the blackness from overwhelming me.

She started to tremble again, this time in real fear.

Suddenly I realized that I enjoyed playing the bully. I abruptly relaxed the pressure.

"OK!" she said. "OK! I'll tell you anything."

"The Nasty Gnomes—who are they?"

"I don't know."

I squeezed again, ever so slightly.

"No, no, *really*! I really *don't* know."

"Who would?"

"Uh, uh, John might…."

"John who?"

"John Ball, my partner. He performs as Tiny Troubles."

"He's a gnome?" I asked.

"No, of course not! He's a Little Person. He's perfectly normal."

"Where can I find him?"

"He lives—he lives a few blocks from here." She gave me the address. "He shares his rooms with several other men. Please don't—don't hurt them!"

I couldn't risk remaining there much longer. I put enough pressure on her neck to make her pass out again, and then quickly departed before she could wake up and start screaming.

But when I reached the safety of the night down below, I realized that, although her bedroom was now displaying a lone beacon of hope, the darkness still spoke to me as silently as death itself. Interesting that she hadn't called the police! I watched her residence for just a moment more, and then vanished down the street, letting the black vapors fill my soul.

It was late, I was tired, and I couldn't besiege John Ball until I had a better idea of his surroundings. I went back to my suite in the Brockleigh-Greeneleaffe Building, and stole some shabby shut-eye from Mr. Sandman.

* * * * * * *

The morning rags were all trumpeting the story: Jacob Wilhelm had tendered his resignation overnight, assuming the blame for the public relations and political fiasco that had occurred the previous day in Harlem. For although the ex-Commissioner had been recovered alive and intact, the city had apparently lost the million dollars that it had ventured on the game—and the kidnappers had all escaped, those who weren't killed. The only question now was whether some official higher up on the administrative ladder would also have to fall on his sword to appease the roaring masses.

I scanned the pages while sipping some tea laced with the South American herb, guarana. I badly needed a pick-me-up this morning. Moco brought me a fried egg-and-ham sandwich, and I munched on that while mulling over our situation.

I hadn't really learned very much from Ruby Diamond, but damn, it had felt good to be taking action again. I'd spent too much time sitting on my ass of late. I worked better when I was causing things to happen.

Franky Castelluccio phoned me at seven o'clock. Thankfully, he had *not* been involved in the assault on the complex, and so had been spared any injury.

"They just keep finding more bodies, sir," he said. "It's horrible down here. Some of our crews in the tunnels were also attacked by the little monsters, and were cut up pretty badly. We estimate fifty, maybe a hundred of the gnomes were killed, but we've found no complete bodies, just miscellaneous pieces—and one head, very badly burned. The death docs are having a field day with it."

"Well, keep me informed as best you can," I said.

I finished my breakfast and walked over to the window. It was still dark outside, and the day looked to be damp and drear. According to the papers, the storm system that had been lingering over the Midwest was now heading for New York, and the forecasters were predicting snow by the afternoon. I was still stiff and creaky from my injuries and my nightly excursions in the cold, and thought about retreating back to bed.

Dastrie appeared a few minutes later. She looked as weathered and worn as I felt, having spent the night in the hospital with her parents.

"How's your father?" I asked.

"He's going to be all right," she said, "but they're keeping him for observation for another day or two. He's dehydrated and hungry and badly bruised. Nothing serious."

"You look all-in."

"So do you," my wife said. She sighed, long and loud, covering her mouth with her hand. "We really need to call the Agency together again, Richard."

"We need some hard information first," I said. "Right now, we don't have a viable plan of action." Then I told her about my visit to Miss Diamond during the wee hours of the morning.

"Why did you have to terrorize that poor girl?" Dastrie said, yawning. "Sometimes I think you just enjoy hurting people, Richard."

"Come on, give me a break: I don't really enjoy this kind of thing"—a necessary lie—"but we have to be ruthless if we're going to stop the cycle of violence. Some people won't talk unless you scare them out of their complacency."

"There has to be a better way. Lord, I'm just so tired these days."

"I think you and I need to pay a visit to the FROGgies later this afternoon, and see who's perched on the ole lily pad."

"Can I get some rest first? Please?"

I started to say "no," but then I realized that I needed the sleep as much as she did, so I just nodded my head.

We crashed for four hours, finally rising at noon and eating a lunch of bruschetta and croustades, with some garlic brie, washed down with a pleasant rosé. I finally felt restored again.

"Ready for our next adventure?" I asked, belching slightly.

"I'm still exhausted, Richard," Dastrie said, "but I won't let you go there alone. We don't know what we're going to find."

So an hour later we were standing outside the entrance to the well-kept structure housing the Fraternal Rotary of Gnomes. The organization's offices were located on the first floor, with recreational facilities on the second, and residential areas on the third and fourth levels.

We were greeted by a mini-receptionist housed in a small alcove just inside the main entrance.

"Can I help you?" the attractive Little Person said.

"We'd like to talk to someone in charge," I said.

"And your business is…?"

"The Nasty Gnomes," Dastrie said.

"I'll see if I can find someone. Wait here, please."

Then she left the room and was gone for five minutes. When she returned, she said, "Mr. Smith will see you now. Please follow me."

Smith was a short, rotund, but muscular man some three feet in height. He might have been thirty or forty—it was hard to tell with his miniature double chin.

"I'm the Director of this facility," he said. "What can I do for you?"

I explained who we were. "We've been asked unofficially to help resolve the mystery surrounding the gnomes and their vicious attacks, and we were hoping that you might be able to provide some background information, or possibly point us towards someone in your community who can assist us."

"Well, you can't think *we're* responsible for these crimes," the director said. "I mean, most of us want as little attention as possible. We're appalled at this slight to our race and our condition. I personally doubt any of our folks are involved."

"Why?" Dastrie asked.

"You have to understand that the Little People have been fighting for generations to secure the basic rights that all of you take for granted. And yet we *are* you, in every way except physical size. We're your sons and daughters and grandchildren. Most of us have 'normal'-sized relatives. But we're confined to this ghetto of poor jobs and poor treatment, just because we look different from the rest of you. We don't *feel* differently, let me assure you. We feel every insult and injury, just like regular folks do.

"The Rotary was founded to help our people work and function as normally as possible in society, to assist those with financial and moral and spiritual needs, and to provide psychological support for them when bad things happen.

"And, unfortunately, bad things seem to happen to us at a far greater rate than they happen to you."

"I understand...," I began.

"No, sir, you don't! Not really! You have no concept of what it's like to be an LP. So don't tell me that you do."

"I apologize, Mr. Smith. I intended no insult to you or your people. But we do really need your help, sir. Crimes are being committed by folks looking like you—and you're being blamed for them. How long will it take before innocent members of your society are targeted by mobs of angry citizens?"

"That's what I've been afraid of, Mr. Van Loan," Smith said. "We're contacting all of our members, telling them to lie low for the time being, to take sabbaticals from their jobs, to go into the streets as little as possible. We don't want any more incidents."

"But who *are* these gnomes?" I asked.

"I don't have an answer to that question, any more than you do. I wish I did. All I've heard are, well, certain rumors over the past few months."

"About what?" Dastrie asked.

"About the Little People wanting to become normal-sized. It's pure fantasy, of course: the physiology of what makes *us* miniature versions of *you* is not really understood, but I doubt very much from what I've read that it can be fixed or adjusted—not after the fact, anyway.

"But some of our group are more gullible than others. They'll buy drugs or treatments that they think will add inches to their height. We've always been prone to such nostrums, but they work no better now than they did in the Middle Ages."

"Who's peddling these things?" I asked.

"I don't know for sure. What I heard was that some new lab had found a way to augment the growth of the Little People, to gradually make them 'normal' again, and that all the costs were being covered by a foundation. But I never saw any hard information to confirm the stories. You had to go meet someone, the tale went, and he would interview you to see if you qualified for the process.

"We had a member who was determined to try for the golden ring. I told him over and over again that this was a foolish risk of his health, that he should be satisfied with what he was. But he'd been bullied by the Big People, and was willing to do anything to augment his growth. He made an appointment with the agent—he wouldn't tell me who he was or where they were to meet—and came back the following day, saying that he'd been accepted into the program, and had been given a ticket to report there the next week. It wouldn't cost him a dime, he said.

"He was so happy that I didn't want to discourage him. He was obviously set on doing this no matter what the cost. So I played along and wished him well. I asked him to come see me when he finished the program—he never did, of course. Once again, he wouldn't tell me where he was going, but he flashed in front of my face the paper that he'd been given. I recognized it at once: it was a ticket to Santy's Village."

"Out in Ronkonkoma?" Dastrie asked.

"The very one. There's a branch office of our organization located there, but it's completely separate from this facility. We share the same Board of Directors, but that and the name are the only connections. They have their own administration in place, and we don't really consult with them that much. They do provide year-round jobs for many of our members, however. A charitable organization actually owns the park itself."

"Where does your funding originate?" I asked.

"We get contributions from a variety of sources, but in the end any deficits are made up by the Board of Trustees. They receive their backing, I understand, from the same group that owns the Village. I don't know any more details than that, sorry."

"But surely the Board publishes an annual report?" I said.

"It does, but details such as the source of our operating funds are a closely kept secret, Mr. Van Loan, and not one I'm privy to."

"Who might be?"

"Well, the Board itself, of course. I can provide you with a list of the directors, if you'd like."

"That would be very helpful."

He buzzed his secretary, and a few minutes later Smith handed me the typed copy as we were leaving.

"If I can be of any other assistance...," he said.

"We'll certainly call on you again," I replied.

* * * * * * *

"Do you recognize any of the names on the Board of Directors of the governing foundation for Santy's Village and the Fraternal Rotary of Gnomes?" Dastrie asked.

"You mean The Organization Against Defamation of Little People?" I said. "No, none of these folks are major players in city or state politics, except possibly one: the attorney for the group, R. M. Cohn. I met him here a few days ago."

"Now that's a very strange coincidence," my wife said. "I wonder why he'd be involved with a bunch like this. You know, Richard, we really need someone from within the community of Little Folks to provide us with reliable, unbiased information. I don't know whether to trust Alexander Smith or not—he seems to have a rivalry going with the sister organization in Ronkonkoma—or at least that's the impression I got."

"I did too. I don't want to rely on him as a sole source for our background data on these people. I wonder if Belle could find one of her old comrades-in-arms in the acting community."

I gave her a call, and she agreed to meet us later that afternoon, if the impending storm didn't impact too heavily on transportation.

"I can always take the subway, sweetie," she said. "I'll see if I can't strong-arm someone else to join me."

* * * * * * *

70

But she never arrived on time. The storm that broke over the Big Apple a few hours later did not just consist of snow and ice and wind, but also of murder and mayhem and mass mischief. About two o'clock, just as the first flakes were beginning to drift their way slowly down from the sky, Christmas shoppers on Broadway were simultaneously attacked by hordes of the Nasty Gnomes. Hundreds of the little creatures boiled up from the depths of the sewers and subways and sloughs underneath the streets, and accosted anyone caught in the open.

Those who immediately failed to hand over their money and jewelry were beaten or knifed. Some of the victims were chased into the stores themselves, where the creatures wrecked the displays of yuletide cheer, terrorizing both patrons and clerks alike, although only one person actually died—and that from a heart attack. Some of the imps were outfitted to look like Santa's helpers, as if deliberately to destroy our children's carefully constructed fantasies of conspicuous holiday consumption. And there was no miracle on Thirty-Fourth Street to save the day.

The police responded in force, of course, but there was little they could do. When they massed at one site, the gnomes would quickly slink away into their hidey-holes, dragging their fortunes along with them in burlap sacks, like the dwarves of ancient Norse and German mythology—and then promptly emerge again somewhere else a few moments later. The underground highways they were traveling made them almost invincible. They had now learned to avoid any direct confrontation with the authorities whenever possible.

As soon as we heard the news, we turned on our radio, and listened to the live coverage of the marauding mini-mobs meandering throughout the downtown area.

"What can we do?" Dastrie asked.

"Not much," I said, "At least not now."

The attacks ceased before sundown, but the damage to the body public had already been done. The Mayor made a live announcement declaring a state of emergency throughout Manhattan, and demanding that the Governor call out the National Guard. Citizens were urged to remain in their apartments, and all stores and public facilities were ordered closed, except by special license. Private vehicles were banned from the streets until further notice.

The siege of New York had begun—and although we didn't realize it at the time, the siege of New York had also ended!

* * * * * * *

The subways continued to run unimpeded throughout the day, however, so workers were able to get home unmolested—and only central Manhattan was actually affected by the two-hour rampage of the Nasty Gnomes. By early evening, the streets had quieted again, particularly as the snow continued to accumulate. We had six inches piled high by six o'clock.

Belle Darling finally appeared at the dinner hour with a guest, and they both agreed to join us for Lamb Chops Luxembourg, which our chef, Maclovio "Moco" Húmedo, was then preparing, along with a nopales, tomato, and onion salad in a special vinaigrette-and-olive-oil dressing, and a spicy *albóndigas* soup. It doesn't get much better than that on a chill near-winter's evening.

Her companion was a sixty-year-old Little Person named Bartholomew Bailey.

"But you can call me Bart," he said, hopping onto a chair next to the dining table. "Can somebody get me a cushion?"

Then he proceeded to wolf down a godawful amount of food, more than I could possibly have eaten myself. I don't know where he put it, given his small frame.

He belched once very loudly, and said: "Ah, now that was somethin' else. Haven't had a meal that fine since, well, since I ate at the old oyster house in Boston. They served me a platter full of them crab legs right out of the Atlantic, and topped it all off at the end with a dish of fresh strawberries perched on a newly baked, double-tiered shortcake. Man alive! Hm-um-hm! Say, you folks got any schnapps?" He burped again. "Belle says you were lookin' to hire me, maybe?"

I explained who we were and what we were doing. "What we want to know," I said, "is what's going on with the Little People?"

His expression soured. "Well, now, I couldn't go a-tellin' tales about the LPs," he said. "If anyone ever found out, why, I'd be frozen out of the group for life. You don't understand what it's like for us, livin' in a world where most people either ignore or despise you. The only acceptance you ever get is among your own kind—but there are so few of us that everyone knows everybody else. You can't really keep a secret in a small community."

"But that's what we're counting on," Dastrie said. "You *know* these people, and you know who's behind these crimes—or you know someone who does, and that's the same difference really. We'd make sure you'd be well paid as part of our organization."

"A detective agency?—nah, I don't think so," the little man said in his squeaky voice. "What future could I possibly have here? Going undercover, huh? Look at me, lady: how do you think I could disguise myself?"

"But, dearie, you were able to make a living for decades as a comedian," Belle said. "I know, 'cause I remember you."

"I barely got by most times. You know how hard things were—for all of us. There just aren't that many roles for the Little People."

"If these attacks continue, the Little People are doomed," I said. "Look at what's happening, Bart. Big folks just won't stand for this nonsense, and you know it. We need to find whoever's responsible, and bring this mess to an end before it gets out of hand."

"I don't disagree with you, Mr. Van Loan," Bart said, "but I have to wonder about *my* future, afterwards."

"I can pay you enough money to have a very comfortable retirement."

"Yeah, sir, but where?"

"Anywhere you like," I said. "How about Brazil?"

He picked for a few moments at the *chocolate con almendras* pie that Moco had just served, and then abruptly asked: "How much?"

"Ten thousand?" I replied.

"Done!" He smiled broadly. "What do you want to know?"

Just then Lizzie beeped me: "Sergeant Castelluccio on Line Two, sir."

"Put him on speaker for me. What's up, Franky?" I asked.

"Mr. Van Loan, I just heard that the Mayor has received a new ransom demand of ten million dollars to stop the attacks on the city, to be paid before the start of business Monday morning."

"Do you know whether or not he intends to comply?"

"All I heard was that he's considering it, and we've been asked to prepare contingency plans either way."

"Thanks for letting us know." I cut the connection.

I turned to Bailey: "They're liable to start rounding up all of the Little People and putting them in concentration camps. Folks like Senator McCarthy will lead the way. Do you have any idea how this all got started?"

"Well, sir, about two years ago I began hearin' these tales about how the foundation was reorganizin'. They'd found some major new sponsors or somethin', and several members of the Board were suddenly replaced. The new people weren't all LPs, and many members of the community objected to having normal-sized people as Directors. But they were overruled, and no one protested out loud very much.

"The truth is, the foundation sponsors not only the two offices of the Rotary, but also the Bureau of Upward-Focused Objectives—which consists of Santy's Village in Ronkonkoma and It's a Wee World Park on Coney Island—you know, the one with the inane music and small figures dressed in all sorts of bizarre costumes, going 'round and 'round and 'round in circles. They provide us with many year-round jobs, work that simply isn't available anywhere else.

"The next thing I heard, six months later, was that the Rotary office at Ronkonkoma was lookin' for volunteers to participate in a scientific study. Seems that some lab was developin' a drug that might add an inch or more to the participant's height. And it actually seemed to work! The first few rats through the maze gradually gained anywhere from a half-inch to two inches in stature over the next few months.

"But there were side effects. The drug affected the individuals' metabolism, requirin' greatly increased intakes of carbohydrates, and swellin' their muscles. Some of the volunteers developed serious mood-swings, leading to fights, beatin's, depression, suicide, and irritability. And you had to keep takin' the meds indefinitely, or the benefits slowly vanished.

"So the tests were eventually ended.

"Meanwhile, many of the more prominent members of the LP community again spoke up against what they regarded as the frivolous expenditure of funds on worthless biological experiments. All of this took place privately, you understand, in letters and phone calls and appearances before the Board—but they threatened to go public with their information unless the foundation changed its policies.

"Several of the leaders of this faction mysteriously disappeared within a matter of days, never to be found, and a third member was mugged, dying of his wounds not long thereafter. He blamed Little People for his attack, which horrified the community.

"All this sent the 'Loyal Opposition' underground, so to speak: it scared them mightily. Two of the remainin' leaders, the cousins John Ball and Julian West—who use the stage names Tiny Troubles and Wee Willie Winkie—mostly kept out of sight thereafter. Although they maintained contact with their followers, they apparently ceased active opposition. And at Ronkonkoma, the experiments were resumed once more, this time with a beefed-up version of the enhancement drug.

"More volunteers were recruited, a great many more, although none of them returned to tell their tales. I believe that these participants constitute what you now call the Nasty Gnomes."

"But how does the woman, Ruby Diamond, fit in?" Dastrie asked.

"I think she may be, uh, John's sister or something."

"Oh, really," I said.

So Ruby hadn't been completely honest with me after all!

"Yes, but you'd have to talk to them yourself, 'cause I don't know her personally," Bart said.

But the club had been closed down with the rest of the city that night, by the snow and the emergency, so I knew we'd have to postpone any further meeting with Ruby and her two companions until another time. As long as the weather continued to worsen, all of us remained *de facto* prisoners of Manhattan.

I sent Belle and Bart home, and Dastrie phoned the hospital to check on her father's condition.

"He's much better," she said smiling, when she returned. "He's apparently sitting up and eating. I wish I could go to him tonight."

"Maybe tomorrow," I said.

Then we retired to our suite to get some additional shut-eye. I knew we'd have little time for sleep later on, once events starting picking up again—and they would, very quickly.

CHAPTER SEVEN

LOOKING BACKWARD
▲
On no other stage are the scenes shifted with a swiftness so like magic as on the great stage of history when the hour strikes.
—Edward Bellamy
▼

NEW YORK, NEW YORK
SATURDAY-SUNDAY, 19-20 DECEMBER 1953

The city remained shut down all day Saturday, as the snow continued to accumulate, finally topping off at thirteen inches. On Sunday the National Guard began to arrive, deploying throughout the downtown area, setting up emplacements and guard stations at key intersections and at all the major department stores. The Mayor announced on radio and television that the shops would reopen as usual on Monday morning, and that holiday patrons would be "absolutely safe and secure."

"You betcha," Dastrie said to me around the breakfast table that Sunday morning, her fork buried deep within the gooey yellow bowels of a soft-boiled egg. "Gad, I seem to be hungry these days. Let me have another, Moco, if you would, please."

"*Sí, Señora.*"

"Yes, all the people are going to be safe and secure—and far, far away from central Manhattan, I can guarantee."

"You're probably right. And I predict that the stock market will nosedive tomorrow as well."

"Do you think the city will pay the ransom?"

"I doubt it," I said. "They've been burned once already, and they can't afford another public debacle. No, they'll take a firm line now—but I'm sure that's precisely what the gnomes, or whoever's behind them, are expecting. The little buggers would have certainly taken the millions if they'd been offered them, but they've already got a million to use in their financial manipulations—and that's exactly what they'll do.

"They've made their point—with an exclamation mark. And the Christmas shoppers certainly got their message: stay away from the stores or risk your lives! The Mayor can post a thousand soldiers on each and every block, but it won't bring the people back downtown. This season has already become an economic disaster."

I sighed.

I'd had quite enough—of breakfast, of discussion, of our inactivity in the face of adversity—and I said so. "I'd really like to get out and shoot some bad guys."

"Just like the old days, Richard?" Dastrie said. "I've heard about the things you did. My father used to tell me. He said that criminals couldn't hide behind corrupt judges and crooked cops while The Phantom Detective was in town. But he also said that he couldn't condone someone who operated outside the law. Times have changed, husband."

"I know they have—you don't have to keep telling me—but I would really like to shoot someone just about now."

Instead, I made discretion the better part of valor, and went to the gym to do my exercises and take a long, very hot shower. The aches and pains from the beating I'd suffered at the hands of the Nasty Gnomes were finally beginning to abate.

I was getting too old for this shit. Maybe it really *was* time for me to retire.

I went to my office, and I hadn't been behind my desk for more than fifteen minutes when there was a timid rap-rap-rap on my chamber door. I immediately pulled an automatic out of the top drawer and flipped off its safety.

I knew Dastrie was still taking a leisurely bath in our living quarters upstairs, and there should have been no one else in the building on a Sunday morning other than the security staff at the main entrance, and the few domestics we kept on the permanent payroll—and the latter were all upstairs. I tripped a silent alarm to alert my wife, and also opened a one-way intercom connection with our living quarters, so she could hear whatever transpired.

"Come in!" I said.

The door slowly creaked open, and what looked like a child's head peaked carefully around the edge.

"Don't shoot, mister! Please don't shoot! I'm…I'm not one of them! Really and truly!

"Are…are you Mr. Van Loan?" the high-pitched voice asked.

"And who are *you*?" I said, motioning the little man inside.

He crawled up on the chair in front of my desk.

"My name is Yulie West," he said. "Someone said you were looking for me."

"*Julian* West? You don't look much like the Froggy or Toady I saw the other night."

"We both wear masks and makeup on stage. The focus is always on Ruby anyway. She's the only one the men watch."

"I was told that you two lead the group opposing the current administration of The Organization Against the Defamation of Little People."

"We disagree with the…with the direction of the new Board of Directors. Encouraging the LPs to believe in body augmentation is just plain wrong. The experiments being conducted are damaging our image and our reputation—and undoubtedly harming the individuals involved. I also think some…perhaps many of the participants have been forced into becoming guinea pigs for unscrupulous experimenters."

"Then for God's sake, why don't you say so publicly?"

"We've been warned…all of us have been warned that anyone who speaks to the press or the police will be killed—or their families will be murdered in their place. We've seen what the renegades can do."

"I thought the Little People had some sort of code of honor to help each other."

"The Little People…the Wee Folk are no different from Big People," he said. "We have good individuals and bad. Some of us will sell themselves for a dollar, and others remain faithful to the old ways. I represent those who honor our ancient traditions of service to King and Goddess. The drama you saw the other night presents our culture in musical form.

"But even the…even the tainted ones would not kill other LPs without extreme provocation, and that's coming from somewhere else—we don't know where. The experiments were first presented to us as a gift from our normal-sized benefactors, and they did seem to help—even *I* tried the first drug, although I should have known better. We all…all of us should have known better. You Big People have always abused us whenever possible. Bullies will ever pick on the weak and defenseless."

"Not all of us are bullies"—another prevarication.

"No, but…but there are enough of you to make our lives miserable; you do the same with the blacks and Jews and others."

"You mentioned some gnome King—is *he* the one who's mounting these attacks?"

"They would have you believe so. They…they will always blame us for everything. But I know the King of the Gnomes personally, and he is *not* that man."

"Then tell me about him."

"You've already…you've seen him at the nightclub. He's my cousin, Johann von Zahl, also known as John Ball or Prince Johann or Tiny Troubles. He was elected King Zähler LXXVII by the Assembly of the Little People five years ago."

"And Ruby Diamond?"

"She…she is his normal-sized half-sister, Princess Rubestra von Zahl. She became Rübezahl, Queen of the Underworld, when Johann was made King. Some of our people regard her as the Living Embodiment of the Goddess of the Gnomes. They will reign jointly until one of them dies."

"Somebody calling himself One-Eye, King of the Gnomes, threatened me down in the old sewer tunnels."

"The renegades have made this man their King, contrary to all our laws and traditions. But this…this abomination may not even be an LP."

"He's a normal-sized man?" I asked.

"We don't know for sure. He…he will not show himself to the rest of the People. He has something to hide. He will lead us all to destruction. If he's a Big Person, he cannot legally be King. Only the Queen can be full-sized under our laws. But he has made himself both King and Queen. He's an abomination."

"But who is he?"

"No one…I don't know his true name. He calls himself One-Eye, and his subordinates Two-Eyes, Three-Eyes, and Four-Eyes. I first heard of him a few years ago. They say that he's the man behind the experiments, that he's the one running the foundation, that he has brought this evil upon the People. He must be destroyed."

"If you won't speak out, what good are you?" I asked.

"We can muster all…every one of the fighters among us, those who would stand up and be counted; and we can lead your men and our soldiers to the heart of the running sore in Ronkonkoma, so that the wound can be lanced and healed for once and for all.

79

THE NASTY GNOMES, BY ROBERT REGINALD

"But there is another place, another axis, though we know not where it is; we must use the knowledge that we gain at the first site to find the second—or the evil will come again, worse than before.

"This…this is what we can do for you—by the word and by the command of Julius, Fürst von Zahl und von Kurzvolk, and in the name of my cousins, King Zähler LXXVII and Queen Rübezahl."

Then he curled his two hands into tight fists, and bringing them abruptly together at his forehead, bowed deeply before me. I bowed to him in turn.

"I accept your offer," I said. "We'll support each other, so that the dignity and safety of the Little People and the Big People can be restored. But before we take any action, we need to reconnoiter the site. We'll go to Ronkonkoma together, and then see what's possible. Agreed?"

"Agreed," he said.

We shook hands to cement the bargain, and he gave me a phone number through which he could be contacted, day or night. Then he left. I never did find out how he'd entered the building unobserved.

When Dastrie appeared a few minutes later, she said: "That was unexpected."

"I think that you and I and the Prince really need to pay a visit to Santy's Village, and see how the elves are doing!"

"What a delightful suggestion. Shall I wear my fur hat?"

"You can wear any damn thing you please," I said. "But fur certainly becomes you."

"It feels like we're moving forward again," she said.

But in my heart of hearts, I still wanted to shoot some really bad people really bad, and I didn't particularly care at this point whether they were the large critters or the small.

CHAPTER EIGHT

JOLLY OLE SAINT NICK
▲

A good many things go around in the dark besides Santa Claus.
—Herbert Hoover
▼

NEW YORK, NEW YORK
MONDAY, 21 DECEMBER 1953

By Monday morning the major city streets had been cleared of both snow and gnomes, and the sun was glittering brightly off the ice-rimed castles of Manhattan. On the surface, at least, things were getting back to normal, if one ignored the ever-present armed National Guardsmen and the beefed-up police patrols. The worker drones were returning in their hordes, each going dutifully to their cells, and only the holiday shoppers seemed conspicuous by their absence.

I phoned Yulie, and we decided to meet at Pennsylvania Station. He was waiting for us there near the ticket counter.

"There's a 10:03 to Ronkonkoma," he said.

We were traveling via the Long Island Railroad, which provided service all the way out to the end of the island.

At this time of the day, the passenger cars were relatively uncrowded, and we sat back to enjoy the scenery as we passed over the East River and entered the suburbs. The towns rolled by, their trees cloaked in furry garments of snow, the roads still shrouded in drifts. What had once been open countryside in my youth was now increasingly populated with upstart housing developments. I wondered if I would live long enough to see every last space within a twenty-mile radius of downtown Manhattan completely obliterated by the continued expansion of the municipal population.

"What can you tell me about Santy's Village?" I asked Yulie.

81

"It was founded in 1939 by a coalition of prominent LPs and a handful of BP benefactors," he said. "They solicited funds from the Rockefellers, from the Mayor, from Wall Street, and from several charitable foundations. The intent was to provide year-round employment for the numerous members of our community who had no jobs—and no prospect of getting any through normal means, particularly during the Depression.

"The land for the site was donated by the philanthropist György Dohanyos, who owned several large estates near Ronkonkoma. We had to have a facility located near enough to the rail line to provide ready access to potential patrons. Alver M. Rockefeller was the key in arranging for the construction of the park proper, which at the time consisted only of the main Village building and separate dormitories for the employees.

"Alver M. Rockefeller?" Dastrie said. "I don't think I've heard of that one."

"That's because he was a Little Person. His family was so ashamed of him that they kept him hidden away—almost a prisoner, in fact—on one of their large country estates. Duke, as he was known, wasn't allowed even to venture outside of the main gate—but he did maintain an active correspondence, and contributed start-up funds for many different projects that benefited our people. He's one of our great heroes."

The train stopped at every village along the way, so our passage out of the city was measured in small stutter-steps. Finally I heard the conductor shout, "Next Stop, Ronkonkoma," as we gradually slowed for yet another station.

We popped out onto the freezing platform, and immediately spotted a shuttle labeled "Santy's Sleigh" slumped over to one side. Red-faced children and puffing parents were just emerging from the open doorway of the bus, their eyes and cheeks aglow with all the fun-fun-fun they'd experienced, many of them carrying candy canes and bags of gaily-wrapped presents.

"Well, they do seem to be a happy bunch," I said.

"We put on a good show," Yulie replied. "My people had to learn very early how to become professional entertainers, and they've done well by it."

We boarded the transport and settled in behind the driver, who was dressed in a red-and-white Santa suit. When everyone was safely seated, he starting yelling "Ho, ho, ho" the minute we pulled out. I could have strangled the bastard after a few minutes: he just wouldn't stop! We traveled several miles through the countryside before reaching the flashing red-and-green lights that signaled—ho, ho, ho!—Santy's Village.

There the bus drove under the arch and creaked to a halt in front of the main entrance. We each ponied up the standard admission fee for adults at the ticket booth, and then stepped into the warm embrace of the main hall.

There we were greeted by the open maw of a massive brick fireplace flanked by black metal andirons in the shape of reindeer. It must have been ten feet high and eight feet wide. Several large logs were burning in the very heart of the hearth, roasting the chestnuts of anyone who ventured too near. I must say, though, that my chestnuts really needed roasting by this time, and I spent a good ten minutes warming my buns while admiring Dastrie's complement of same. I think Prince Julius was getting quite exasperated with us by this time.

"I could really use some lunch," my wife finally said. "I seem to be hungry all the time."

Yulie sighed and pointed off to one side of the great-room, where another open archway was labeled "Mrs. Claus's Kitchen."

"Sounds good to me," she said. "Lead on!"

I needed to locate another kind of facility first, but I joined them a few minutes later after taking care of business.

"What's on the menu?" I asked.

"I recommend the Portuguese Sausage and Kale Soup," the little man said. "It includes Lingüiça, onions, garlic, kale, olive oil, and rice, among others, and is just delicious on a wintry day. That's what I'm having, with a toasted Pimento Cheese Sandwich."

"Victor's Chili looks pretty good to me," Dastrie said. "I wonder who Victor was."

"Just some old hack, I think," the Little Person said. "He carved his name into several of the tomes around here."

"Anyway, I think I might try that—and also the Endive, Stilton, and Bacon Salad."

"They've got Crab Cakes!" I said. "I love good shellfish. I'll order that together with Chicken Chasseur and Gratin Dauphinois. And how about Fig and Cocoa Sugar Plums for a seasonal dessert, folks?"

"Drinks, lady and gentlemen?" the waiter asked.

"A Dorothy Parker," Yulie said.

"Ooh, hot eggnog for me," Dastrie said.

"And a Mimosa for *moi*," I added.

I looked around the room for the first time. The ceiling was supported by several huge, blackened cross beams of thick wood. Small latticed windows overlooked the open fields at the front of the structure.

Then I noticed the two individuals seated at a table on the far side of the room, their heads almost touching as they leaned forward in earnest conversation. One of them was Alexander Smith, the Director of the Rotary facility in Harlem. The other was R. M. Cohn, the attorney for the foundation that operated Santy's Village.

I nudged Dastrie, and nodded at the pair across the way.

"That's the lawyer I told you about," I said.

"He's on the foundation Board of Directors," Yulie said, "but he doesn't seem to participate actively in its proceedings, from what I hear."

"Then I wonder what he's doing here now. You know, I think I'll go ask him."

I ambled slowly in and around the scattered tables, not obviously heading in their direction—until I suddenly pounced.

"Gentlemen," I said, "How good to see you both again. You didn't strike me as the Christmassy type."

Both of them suddenly looked as if they'd stuffed themselves with way too much pasta.

"Uh, Mr. Van Loan," Cohn said. "What are you doing here?"

"I think that's my question."

"I'm legal advisor to the Board of Directors, and this is official foundation business—not that it's any of *your* business!"

"And Mr., uh, Smith, isn't it?" I said. "Sounds like a *nom de guerre* to me. I thought you didn't get along with the folks here in the Village."

"There are occasions, Mr. Van Loan, when one must consult with one's superiors."

"So Mr. Cohn's your superior now, eh?" I was thoroughly enjoying this little *tête-à-tête*.

"He's certainly one of them."

"Then who is Number One?" I asked.

"Sorry I'm late," a third voice interjected.

I looked around. A normal-sized woman of about sixty was standing there, impatience etched on her brow. She had a pinched, pockmarked face, slashed gray hair pulled into a stern bun, and a permanent, disapproving frown stitched forever on her thin lips.

"And just who are *you*?" she demanded. She acted as if the place was leased to her permanently.

"Richard Curtis Van Loan, madame," I said, bowing. "And you are...?"

"Eulalie Jeanne Doyenne. I'm the Chairman of the Board, as well as the Director of Santy's Village and Alver's Avowers, our booster boys."

"Just the person I wanted to see! I and my associates are looking for a worthy charity in which to invest our funds, and I was told of the good work that both the Village and the Rotary have been accomplishing these past few years. We really want to aid your cause."

"Well, uh, of course, Mr. Van Loan. I've certainly heard your name. I mean, everyone knows about Van Loan Enterprises and the benefits that you endow. We would, uh, we'd greatly welcome your financial support."

"I've already met with Mr. Smith here," I said, nodding in his direction, "and also with Mr. Cohn. I was greatly impressed with everything they told me. But we cannot, as you might imagine, proceed without some additional information, so we wanted to view the facilities for ourselves. I was wondering if you could possibly provide us with a personally guided tour of the entire enterprise after we finish our luncheon."

"Why, I...I would be honored," she said, batting her ugly eyes, in just the same way, I would imagine, as Medusa did before freezing her victims into stone. I had to force myself not to shudder.

"And who is accompanying you?" She squinted across the room at my two companions.

"Ah, that's my dear wife, Dastrie Lee Underhill Van Loan, and our friend, the well-known comedian, Wee Willie Winkie."

"Oh, well, of course they can come too. Just give me a 'yoo-hoo-ee' when you're ready, and I'll clear my slate this afternoon."

"Thank you so much, Miss Doyenne." I bowed again. "Gentlemen, it's been a pleasure encountering you once more."

When I sauntered back to our table, the food was being served, and I took time between bites to bring my colleagues up-to-date.

Alas, the crabby cakes were rather dry and flaky, not at all like the moist renditions served at Le Gnome Gastrique.

"How's your chili?" I asked my wife.

"H-h-hot! But very tasty."

I also tried a sip of Yulie's soup, which was over-salty to my mind, but still quite spicy and ultimately satisfying. My chicken was tender and well-seasoned, and the portabellas out of this world. However, the sudsy spuds were a bit overcooked and mushy. I did enjoy the unusual treat of the sugar plums; the figs gave them a very tasty twist.

When we were finished, I asked for the bill, but the waiter said, "Not to worry, sir, Miss Doyenne has taken care of it."

"We should have ordered more!" Yulie said, burping.

"We've probably had enough. Let's go see what this place has to offer," I said, pushing back my chair.

Eulalie Jeanne Doyenne met us at the restaurant entrance. "If you'll follow me," she said.

The primary structure had been originally built as a long, two-story building, containing the restaurant, large hall, meeting rooms, and Santa's Home on the first floor, and the Santa Claus Museum, Director's Office, and Santa's Workshop on the second. After the war, the foundation added two wings, forming the letters "T" on either end, to provide rooms for paying guests who wanted to remain overnight. As more buildings were added to the site, Santa's Workshop and Home were moved elsewhere, and the Museum was expanded across the entire top level of the main structure, plus a newly added gift shop. The original Santa's Home was remodeled into a plush administrative office suite.

We walked all around and through the building, but it was nothing more than it seemed. The Museum displayed interesting artifacts relating to Santa Claus and Christmas dating back into the nineteenth century. The gift shop peddled cheap curios and a few genuine antiques at overinflated prices.

The main tourist attractions, however, were located out back.

Santa's Home was a separate brick structure off to the left; it looked like a cross between a gingerbread house and something out of the Brothers Grimm, with bright red walls with brown trim, and a deliberately crooked chimney. Good old Santa himself was present to greet us out front, of course, along with Mrs. Claus and all of the attendant slave laborers (the omnipresent elves). The kiddies just ate it up, although I quickly tired of the incessant "Ho, ho, ho!"-ing.

Santa's Workshop, a long, rattletrap barracks of a building, was situated behind and to the right. Through the wide open doorway we could espy dozens of the little buggers pounding away on faux machinery in the huge single room. They raised such a clanging and banging to the heavens that even the dead might have fled the place. It wasn't quite clear to me what they were creating, although the end product—piles of gaily wrapped (but rather small) Christmas packages—were stacked to either side. Each child who visited the place was allowed to choose one of these cheap toys to take home.

The Reindeer Stable had been erected to the right rear of the entrance hall, and consisted of open pens and a large barn that housed living examples of the deer-like creatures, along with Clydesdale horses, caribou, and elk. I wasn't exactly sure how the Clydesdales fit in with the Christmas story.

To the left rear of Santa's Home we saw an artificial grotto displaying the nativity scene of the baby Jesus, complete with Mary and Joseph and little James (Jesus's brother), images of the three wise men—Caspar, Balthazar, and Melchior—real sheep and goats, and another complement of elves. The Little People were everywhere. The small adjoining chapel of St. Lambert, adorned with a Maltese cross, had obviously been erected to allow individuals of various Christian denominations to pause and reflect on the over-commercialization of the holiday season—but not for long!

Behind Santa's Workshop we spied several of the cheap wood dormitories that housed the employees—each contained fifty small one-room apartments, a cafeteria, and a recreational room. Nearby was the physical plant that provided heat and power for the site, plus a small, single-story wood structure sheltering the local Rotary office.

There was nothing else visible—and no place, really, in which to secrete any other facility. Everything was just as it seemed.

"Well, Mr. Van Loan," Miss Doyenne said, "What do you and your committee members think?"

"Oh, we're quite, quite impressed," I allowed. "It's rare that we find such a highly organized and efficiently run amusement park."

"It's more than just play, Mr. Van Loan—it's instructional too! The children are taught all about the basic values of Christmas and the holiday spirit."

"I can certainly see the lessons they're being given here," Dastrie said.

"What about the Little People?" I asked.

"We employ more than a hundred of them during the Fall and Winter months, and about half that number the rest of the year. They're required to live on site, of course, and to pay for their room and board out of their wages."

"That's certainly convenient, isn't it?"

"Indeed it is. And they do so benefit from the programs and training that we provide them."

"I notice that the Rotary office here is quite small, just three or four rooms in a fairly modest structure," I said.

"Well, that's because it's a branch of the main facility in New York City."

"I thought it was separately run."

"Oh, no, not at all. There's a local manager present, of course, but he reports directly to the administrator in Harlem."

"Alexander Smith?"

"Yes. Mr. Smith's been in charge for, I would guess, maybe three years."

"What did he do before that?" Yulie asked.

"I think he was an entertainer, like so many of the LPs. But it's a hard life, and not many of them can make a living at it."

"Did he have a stage name?"

"I'm sure he did—they all did—but I don't recall it now, if I ever knew it. That was before my time, you know," she simpered.

We were walking across one of the plowed pathways criss-crossing the quad area behind the main building when it happened. A loud crack sent everyone diving to the ground. I pulled my snub-nosed .38 from its hidden holster on my calf, but I couldn't see where the shooter was hiding.

I heard a groan nearby, and turned my head. Eulalie Jeanne Doyenne had been shot in the left side, and was bleeding lovely pink streamlets onto the snow. They looked almost like Christmas decorations.

I rolled over and quickly patted her down. The bullet had glanced off her lowest rib, leaving two flesh wounds. I put my arm under her shoulders, and then led a two-step parade back to the safety of the rear entrance.

"Call an ambulance and the police," I yelled to no one in particular, as I laid my burden down on a couch.

"Oh, it hurts," Miss Doyenne said.

"You're going to be fine, my dear, just fine. There'll be help here soon."

Then I popped out the back door again, dodging screaming parents and their kids while I headed for the stables in a zigzag pattern. The sound of one bullet isn't enough to coordinate the location of a shooter, but the bang had seemed louder to me on the left-hand side of the quad—and the stables would have provided the best cover for a possible assassin.

The culprit was long gone, of course. I found the place where he'd been kneeling, waiting for the opportunity to shoot, and I even located the spot where the still-warm shell casing, a .306 maybe, had burned through the snow. I left it where it had fallen for the police to find. They'd be here soon enough.

More interesting was the message scratched into the pristine snow nearby: "Van Loan: in the Kingdom of the Blind, the One-Eyed man is King." It was taken from an old short story by H. G. Wells. I wiped the words away.

Then I lost the killer's tracks in amongst those of the animals, but from what I could tell, they seemed to represent the stride of a normal-sized person. In any case, no LP would have been able to handle a full-sized rifle without being bowled over by the recoil.

As soon as the cops appeared, we were questioned and questioned and questioned—and finally released after several hours of going nowhere. We took the next Santy Shuttle into town, and boarded the train back to Manhattan.

I asked my companions for their evaluations.

"It's a dead end," Prince Julius was forced to admit. "I have to say I was wrong: there's just no place to hide an operation of the kind we're seeking. I'm truly sorry to have wasted your time, Mr. Van Loan. You must understand that I hadn't actually visited the Village in over a decade."

"You didn't waste anyone's time, Yulie. After all, someone did fire at us. And I don't really think they were aiming at Eulalie Jeanne."

"She was standing right in front of me. Was I the target?"

"Perhaps. But it's also possible that the shooter was simply making a point. Do you have any idea who Alexander Smith was in his earlier incarnation in comedy?"

"I've only heard of him in the context of his current office; I never knew any LP performer named Alexander Smith."

"Who might?"

"My cousin might know something more. He keeps tabs on all of the important people in our community."

"Then I think we'd better interview your cousin—and soon."

"Why is this so important?" Dastrie asked.

"Well, there's something going on here we're just not getting, something essential to understanding the puzzle. I think it all goes back to the Rotary somehow. The gnomes have only been seen in downtown New York, after all. That strongly suggests they're primarily headquartered in the Big Apple, and the main organization of Little People there is the one run by Alexander Smith.

"Santy's Village was a feint designed to take our attention away from the real center of activity. Perhaps they started the experiments here in Ronkonkoma, I don't know. But I think they've progressed beyond that now. I think the answers we're seeking are literally right underneath our noses. They're down there somewhere, and we have to find them and stop them before they attack again."

"I'll arrange for John and Ruby to meet with us tomorrow," Yulie said.

Then the train entered a tunnel, and everything went black.

CHAPTER NINE

THE KING OF HEARTS
▲

Or ever the knightly years were gone
With the old world to the grave,
I was a King in Babylon
And you were a Christian Slave.
                    —William Ernest Henley
▼

NEW YORK, NEW YORK
TUESDAY, 22 DECEMBER 1953

The next morning, I asked Lizzie to arrange for a meeting of the Agency members that afternoon.

Then I phoned Police Sergeant Francesco Castelluccio, and after several tries was finally able to locate him.

"It's a madhouse down here," he said. "Mr. Van Loan, I'm not going to be able to help you much until the crisis eases."

"I know that, Franky. But there's one thing you could do for me that would help. I need to find out whatever you folks have on Alexander Smith, Director of the Harlem office of the Fraternal Rotary of Gnomes."

"That's a fairly common name."

"I realize that, and I also know how busy you are. Just do what you can quickly, and get back to me, please, by one o'clock."

"I'll try."

My second call was to Fast Eddie Underhill, who'd been released from the hospital a few hours earlier, and was now convalescing at home, while keeping in touch with his task force. Dastrie had taken him there with the help of her mother, Zenobia.

"I was sure glad to be let out of that corral," the former Police Commissioner said. "I got real danged tired of the food."

I filled him in on the recent developments.

"My filly's mentioned some of this already, Van. So you think the creatures are still lurkin' somewheres around here?"

"I'm certain of it, and think that there's some personal animus involved as well. The messages that I've been getting aren't just random, Eddie—they were planted for me to find by someone who's been deliberately taunting me. I think we have two crimes here: the attack on me, and the one against the city—the latter being mainly a financial one. Look at how the market crashed yesterday. That was certainly no accident."

"You're right, of course: it was down a hundred points, and seems headed in the same direction today. Somebody's got to be makin' a passel of moola out of all this."

"Whoever's behind your kidnapping has already profited hugely from the attacks. It's only a matter of time before they pull their funds out and retreat into the sewers. If they do, we'll never find them again."

"How much time do you think we have?"

"They'll keep the pressure on through Christmas Eve, the traditional end of the sales season. That gives us two or three days—no more—to track the villains down and bring them to justice. Then Ole Saint Nick will trundle back to the North Pole."

"Well, the Department won't allow me to officially return until the quackers sign off on my health. That'll be tomorrow at the earliest."

I sighed. "I really need your help, Eddie—your *official* help—to bring this case to some kind of closure. I've got an idea of what's going on, but I'm waiting for confirmation. The problem is, when we finally do make our move, we may have to do so in force, because the Nasty Gnomes will fight back with everything they've got. Right now they're being controlled by whoever's behind this mess. If that individual dies or is removed, they might start attacking everyone in sight. We have to prevent that at all costs."

"Do you honestly think they can be cured of whatever's ailin' them?" Eddie asked.

"I believe so, but we have to capture them first, and that's not going to be easy. To do so, we may have to mobilize a large force."

"I don't know: that's a pretty short window, Van."

"The operation will have to take place on Thursday. If you're back at work tomorrow, I think it's at least doable."

"Then I *will* go back, come hell or high water. You have my word on it, ole buddy."

"That's all I ask. Now can I talk to Dastrie?"

When she came on the line, I told her about the meeting that I was setting up for the afternoon.

"I'll be there," she said. "Daddy seems to be doing fine, Richard. He's sore and still a bit shaky, but I think a good night's rest in his own bed and several home-cooked meals are all he really needs."

"I'm glad to hear it. At his age...."

She laughed out loud for the first time in many days. "He's not that much older than *you* are, my dear."

"Too true. Ah, it's good to hear your voice again. Do come home soon."

"I love you too," she whispered, "More than you can ever imagine."

* * * * * * *

My wife returned home just before noon. We popped around the corner to catch lunch at the Brisketeers Café—the thick lentil soup and rare New York steak sandwich topped with grilled onions and mushrooms were well worth the effort, and Dangerous Dave O'Doul, the proprietor, was always there front and center to make certain everything was done right. The sign displaying the Three Briskateers with their spatulas *en garde* never failed to amuse me.

We were back by one-thirty, just in time to greet our comrades-in-arms. Yulie introduced his two cousins, the King and Queen of the Gnomes.

His Royal Highness was about three feet high, slim, and with a slight mustache adorning his upper lip; he might have been forty, though he looked older. His brow was creased with lines of concern.

"Call me John," he said, holding out his hand. "And this is my sister, Ruby."

His normal-sized sibling was both lovelier and livelier, with a sparkle in her eyes that said, "I know what you're thinking—you can look but not touch!" She showed no sign of our little *tête-à-tête* of the previous Friday, other than a scarf wrapped carefully around her throat. If she recognized us from the club, she said nothing.

I welcomed them both to the group, and introduced the others.

Then they took their places at the end of a conference table that included all of the members of The Phantom Detective Agency, East Coast Division, save for Franky Castelluccio.

"We need your help, John," I said. "We have to stop the Nasty Gnomes before they can cause any more havoc. I'd much rather preserve their lives and wean them from their chemical dependency, if I can; but if it comes down to a choice between innocent people being slaughtered and the death of any Gnome—well, I want you to know that there *is* no choice in my own mind. This scourge must cease immediately."

"I agree," the monarch said. "We'll help in any way we can."

"Good. Let's try to coordinate our efforts with the police as well.

"It seems to me that the key to this entire affair lies at the door of the Fraternal Rotary of Gnomes. The question is: who is Alexander Smith, where did he originate, and how did he become Director of the organization?

"This morning I asked Sergeant Castelluccio to dig into Smith's background. He phoned me back a few minutes ago. Franky discovered that Smith was born in 1920 at Round Top, New York. It's a village lying about halfway between Albany and Poughkeepsie, some miles west of the Hudson River.

"What *I* find interesting about this particular datum is that I myself was born just a few miles distant from there, albeit at an earlier date, and I was raised on a large estate flanking the nearby waterway. But I'd left home by the time Smith was born in 1920, so I've never heard of this family. What possible connection, if any, can there be between us?

"When we questioned Miss Doyenne, the Manager of Santy's Village, *she* said that Smith had previously worked as an entertainer under a stage name—a name she didn't know. So who was Alexander Smith *before* he became Director of the Rotary?"

"Well, Mr. Van Loan," John Ball said, "I checked on this after Yulie told me of your concern, and I found him listed in one of our old record books. Smith used the stage name Petite Souris for about a decade."

"Oh, I remember him," Belle Darling said. "People in the business called him 'Petey.' In the late 1930s and early '40s he used to play a ventriloquist's dummy in a comedy act."

"A ventriloquist's dummy?" Dastrie asked. "You're kidding."

"Yeah, it was a joke, dearie. They'd dress him up in a mask and suit, and he'd sit on a hidden stool next to the entertainer, who would appear to have his hand up the doll's back—and Petey would move and act just like, well, just like a dummy, but would make the appropriate responses through his own mouth. And then, at the end of the skit, he'd suddenly jump up and walk across the stage—and everyone in the club would be absolutely flabbergasted. Afterwards

94

he'd come out and take his bow, and they'd all start laughing and clapping.

"This went on for, oh, maybe seven or eight years, until one day the ventriloquist, an old alky named Justus Goebel, farted right in the middle of the act—I mean, a big, loud, smelly stinko of a stench. Then the whole theatre suddenly went silent, just for a moment—until the audience started laughing, and wouldn't stop. Even 'Just' joined in—couldn't help himself. Every time things started to settle down, they'd start guffawing again. And then Petey, well, he just jumped up from his stool and walked away—and never came back! Said he'd had enough of being humiliated. I don't know what happened to him after that—I never saw him again."

"Do you know if Smith was his birth name?" I asked.

"No," several voices echoed, including John and Belle.

"I only know of Souris's connection with Smith," the King said, "because of the registration book we try to maintain, listing the major LPs in the New York metropolitan area. It's never complete, of course, but it's the only way we have of tracking our people coming and going, particularly those who employ pseudonyms in the entertainment industry, or those who need our help. Petey's surname was listed as Smith by the time he became a performer at the age of seventeen—in 1937."

"Both of you pronounce his name with a terminal 'S', as if it were Greek in origin," I said. "But how do you actually spell it?"

"The book listed it as S-O-U-R-I-S," John said.

"But that could be pronounced 'Sou-RI'," Dastrie interrupted.

"Indeed it could. Hmm, I wonder...," I said.

"Wonder *what*, Richard?"

"I'll need to make another phone call, and then we'll see. But I can do that after our meeting. First I need to know, Cullen, who's been doing what to the financial markets."

"Well, as you suspected," the pawn shop owner said, "A secret hand has been at work behind the scenes, speculating on futures and transferring funds back and forth in and out of the stock market. This started on Friday...."—*"Friday!"* Quent interjected—"...Yes, Friday! Actually, Friday morning, to be precise, before the ransom was paid and Mr. Underhill was released. You can do a great deal on spec, if you know the right people, and if those people are confident you can pay.

"They're operating as the Norry Sumach Co., which was registered as a corporation under New York law a week ago. It appears to be one of a series of shell businesses that would take forever to track down."

"So who are the officers of this new firm?" I asked.

"They're the same as the officers of all the other companies connected with this organization—mostly attorneys and accountants with mail-drop addresses. There are corporate lawyers who make a living from just doing this sort of thing—setting up dummy structures to fool the tax men and the federal and state regulators. If one of the businesses is caught hanging over the line, they cut off that particular appendage, and let it die the death of obsolescence. Suddenly the bogus outfit disappears, leaving no assets, and another is immediately put in its place.

"It's all technically legit, and all very hush-hush. It's just how some rich men get richer.

"Anyway, this Norry Sumach Co. has been trading very quickly and successfully these past few days, transferring funds in and out of banks in New York at a rapid pace, and shifting some of its assets to Switzerland. Whoever's doing this really knows their stuff—this is no amateur at work, Mr. Van Loan."

"How much do you think they've made?"

"Can't say for sure, but certainly in the multiple millions. You'd be amazed at what you can do with a little advance knowledge."

"And by manipulating the public," Dastrie said.

"Indeed."

"How do we stop them?" I asked.

"Well, I'm not sure that we can," Cullen said. "Not legally, anyway. If you tried to get someone to open an official investigation, why, they'd vanish right before your eyes. You'd never see them again, and their attorneys would claim that they were acting on behalf of *other* corporate clients, and so on and so on, *ad infinitum*. You'd never reach the end of the train."

"But someone *is* listed with the State of New York as Treasurer or Chief Financial Officer of the corporation, isn't that correct?"

"Yes, it's, uh, let me see, I've got it here somewhere. Oh, yes, it's Raúl Luis Villa Mendosa, the Treasurer. He's got an office in a building on 111th Street. That's not a good area of town, you know."

"Well, I've got an idea of how we could disrupt some of the plans of the Norry Sumach Co., whomever or whatever they might represent. Of course, it might not be entirely kosher, if you know what I mean. I wouldn't ask any of you to participate unless you understand the risks. If we're caught, you could be arrested and prosecuted."

I looked around the table. Each of them nodded in turn.

"For this particular adventure, I'll need Cullen, for your financial know-how; Zinc and Rubio, for your muscle; and Quent, for your knowledge of locks and safes. We'll do it tonight, as soon as it gets dark. It's time to resurrect The Phantom Detective, folks, and finally take some positive action to close this case."

* * * * * * *

The Segue Building was an elderly three-story brownstone that had been subdivided at some point in its not-so-sterling history into one- and two-room offices. Since the structure hadn't really been designed for such use, access to the upper levels was awkward at best, being gained through a scratched wooden staircase covered with frayed blue carpet.

Half of the rooms in the place were apparently vacant, while the others housed a cleaning service, a detective agency, and a rent collector. Villa Mendosa's door on the third story was as tired as all the rest, with a slab of opaque glass layering the upper half, and the words "V.M. Financial" stenciled across the middle in faded gold letters.

At five P.M., the rest of the doors were closed and locked, and their owners gone off to wherever failed businessmen gather at night. But a light still showed behind the entrance to #9. Raúl Luis Villa Mendosa was working late this evening!

I nodded to my crew, and we slipped the masks up over our faces, pulled down the brims of our hats, and grabbed our automatics. Then we quietly entered through the front door.

A faint tinkling of a distant bell announced our arrival.

"*¿Sí, señores?*" came a voice from the back room.

I nodded to Cullen to latch and watch the entrance, and then pushed open the hatch to the inner sanctum.

"What ees it you want?" the little man said.

He sported a narrow, neatly trimmed mustache under tired eyes and a swatch of greased-back, coal black hair. Then he saw our guns and masks.

"I have no *dinero* here, *señores, nada!*"

I pulled up a chair and sat astride it facing him across his desk.

"Keep your hands where I can see them, Raúl Luis," I ordered. "Or you may develop a sudden disability.

"You're the Treasurer of one of my favorite corporations, and I don't think that I even have to tell you what it is. I would like to make a little investment in the future, and I understand that you specialize in financial matters of all kinds."

"I don't what you mean, *señor*."

"Of course you do," I said, pointedly pointing my automatic right at his heart. "You've spent the last few days making loads of money for some of my friends, and I've decided that it is exceedingly unfair of them to have left me out of the equation, so to speak. I'm here to rectify this unkindness."

"I do not understand."

"Oh, but you will. Somewhere you have a register of the transactions you've made on behalf of the Norry Sumach Co. I want it. I also want the bank and other financial account numbers and transfer numbers, plus all the numbers or passwords necessary to access same. Then we're going to play a little game. Do you know what the name of that game is, *señor*?"

Villa Mendosa was looking decidedly pale by this time.

"N-no," was all he could say.

"It's called 'Find the Money'. We're going to find *all* the money, and then we're going to move it somewhere else."

"No, no, no, you cannot do that," the little man said. "They will kill me if...."

"I will kill you now if you don't," I said, waving my weapon in a circle. "If, on the other hand, you cooperate, I will facilitate your impending retirement by providing you with a plane ticket to Brazil, plus enough money for you to live comfortably down there. I realize that the language isn't the same, but I'm sure you'll adjust very well. They do say the beaches are quite beautiful this time of the year—not to mention the beach-goers."

He ran a hand across the mop of hair hanging down almost into his eyes. "I...I cannot do thees. You do not know these people. They will track me to the ends of the earth."

"But that is a 'maybe,' Raúl Luis. This..."—I again poked my gat right at his prissy nose—"...Thees ees a certainty. Choose wisely, *mi amigo*. My colleagues and I are getting a bit impatient.

"Perhaps we can help you with your decision. Quent, make sure the blinds cover the windows. Zinc, we need to find the safe and any weapons. Rubio, please tie up *Señor* Villa Mendosa, and then tell this *perro faldero* exactly what's going to happen to him."

The ex-boxer let loose a string of invective that I could only partially follow, and while lashing the treasurer to his own chair, outlined in great and glorious detail all of the tortures, humiliations, and perversities that would be worked upon his lean body if he failed to do everything that "El Fantasma" demanded of him.

"Hee, hee, hee, lookee here, boss," Zinc said, holding up the snub-nosed revolver he'd just pulled from Villa Mendosa's top desk drawer. He stuffed it into his coat pocket. "Got me some paperwork, too." He held up several account books.

"OK, Zinc, let's get Cullen back in here."

When the pawn shop owner appeared, I handed him the registers, and asked him to scour them for any pertinent information. After a few minutes, he looked up and said: "These record the transactions, all right, but they don't provide the numbers that I need to access the accounts."

"You sure this guy has them?" I asked.

"Yeah, he's got 'em stashed somewhere here—has to in order to make the transfers. The guy in charge would also have access to the main accounts—they wouldn't trust someone on this level to manage such things exclusively."

I got up, went around the desk, and then grabbed the accountant by his tie. I yanked up on the cloth until he started to cough.

"We can do this nicely, and we can do it the hard way," I said. "Your choice, *señor. Where are those numbers?*"

"I, I, I…."

"You're, uh, choking him, sir," Quent said in his matter-of-fact way. "We don't want him to die on us just yet."

I abruptly let go, and Villa Mendosa slumped back in his chair again. He was wheezing out loud, drawing these long, deep-down breaths in and out, in and out, of that narrow chest.

"Found the safe, boss," Zinc said from the corner. "It was hidden behind the stained wood wall panel."

"The combination!" I demanded of Raúl Luis. "Now!"

"Dos," he whispered, *"Once, diez y nueve, cuarenta y ocho."*

Rubio translated while Zinc spun the dials.

"Got it," Zinc said, pulling the heavy door toward him.

Inside were bundles of cash tied with string, and several small notebooks, passbooks, and other papers.

"Distribute the money," I ordered Zinc. "Cullen, see what you can make of these documents."

"There's account information for a half-dozen financial institutions, including a Swiss bank, plus all the data we need to facilitate the transactions."

"Excellent. Zinc, please gag *Señor* Villa Mendosa."

Then I dialed our personal telephone number, and when Dastrie answered, gave her the Swiss bank account information and all the other financial names and access codes.

"You know what to do," I said.

It was now almost six o'clock. We had our own accounts in Switzerland, and the financial institutions there opened promptly at three our time.

I next called Fast Eddie at his home, and said: "This is Richard Van Loan. I thought you'd like to know that we've managed to track down the ransom money. Dastrie will be phoning you shortly with all of the relevant data. I'm sure you'll have a good idea of just what to do with it. The City will retrieve everything that it lost—and more—and we'll cripple the operations of the Nasty Gnomes. However, you need to get your people ready for tomorrow, just in case there's a violent reaction from the Gnomes."

"Thanks so much for this, Van. It should provide me with the push I need to get reinstated," he said. "I'm ready to jump back in the saddle again—to finish the job we started!"

"So am I," I said. "So am I."

After hanging up the phone, I turned to Villa Mendosa and pulled the rag out of his mouth: "So, what's it going to be then, eh?"

"You do not know thees man. He will kill me."

"*Who* will kill you?" I asked.

He shook his head. "I, I cannot tell you."

"Whisper it," I ordered, leaning down close to his mouth.

And he named a name that didn't surprise me in the least.

"I'll take care of him," I said, smiling. "Oh, yes, I will make certain that he will trouble you no more, *señor*."

Then I slipped a piece of paper into his pocket. "That's a ticket to Rio on the midnight flight. I would suggest that you might want to get to the airport right away. Here's your passport and $10,000 to get you started." I slapped both down on the desk.

"Release him, Zinc," I said.

Villa Mendosa looked around at us, making little twitchy movements with his head, his eyes like those of a pigeon that has suddenly been cornered by a cat.

"I will do as you say," he said. "But God, He will curse the day you were born, *señor*! *¡Vaya con Diablo!*"

Then he crept out the front door.

"Let's get out of here, gents," I said.

Zinc thoughtfully flicked off the light on our way out.

CHAPTER TEN

THE ZERO ZOMBIES
▲

But never met this Fellow
Attended or alone
Without a tighter breathing
And Zero at the Bone—
—Emily Dickinson
▼

NEW YORK, NEW YORK
WEDNESDAY, 23 DECEMBER 1953

Dastrie and I were up till the wee hours taking care of business overseas, but when we were done, more than two million dollars had been deposited into our secure account in Bern, having been transferred from the Norry Sumach Company's Swiss holdings. I regarded this as nothing more than just payment for our services in the crisis. The city would still get its money back—and then some—from the half-dozen domestic banks in which the NS Corporation maintained a financial presence.

We finally went to bed around three-thirty, having set the alarm clock for six. I'd asked all of the members of our group to assemble at the Brockleigh-Greeneleaffe Building by eight. I was expecting more trouble.

"As soon as they realize what we've done," I told my lovely wife, "they're going to come after us."

"And not just us, I suspect," she said, stifling a yawn. "The police as well, and maybe the downtown shopping areas again."

"Did you arrange for additional guards?"

"They'll be here by seven. And now I really think we need to get some shut-eye."

It seemed as if we had scarcely put heads to pillow before the buzzer went off.

We choked down a light breakfast of bacon, grapefruit, and toast, went through our exercise routines, and took a joint shower—which demonstrated once again just how much fun cleanliness can really be!

Just before eight o'clock, as the members of The Phantom Detective Agency were beginning to appear, I got a phone call from Fast Eddie Underhill.

"I thought you'd like to know," he said, "that I'm back in the saddle once again, pard, fully reinstated. The first thing that I did was to get court orders freezin' the bank accounts of the Norry Sumach Co. They're tied up as tight as two fillies in a horse trailer."

"Great news," I said. "Any idea how much they had stashed away?"

"Several millions, at least. The city will be more than repaid for its ransom money."

"Glad to hear it. You might want to deploy the Guard again throughout the downtown area."

"Already taken care of: they'll be out in force, Van. I've also stationed 'em around Police Headquarters. Just let the little buggers try somethin'. We'll be ready for 'em."

"I'm got extra men posted here too," I said.

"Let me know if you need any help."

One by one our compatriots found their way to the conference table. I'd also invited John Ball, the King of the Gnomes, together with his sister, Ruby Diamond, and cousin, Prince Yulie.

We'd established the additional guards at the main and rear entrances to the building—but the attack, when it came, surprised us once again. The Nasty Gnomes had forced their way into the basement, and then infiltrated the elevator shaft.

I had just opened our meeting when I heard the rat-a-tat-tat of shots being fired on the lower levels.

Zinc quickly handed out weapons to everyone, and we headed into the lobby in front of the lift.

The grotesque little men were just starting to appear, some armed with revolvers, but most just with knives.

"Lizzie!" I shouted, "Call the cops!"

Two of the gnomes suddenly dashed into the main lobby of our third floor office suite, heading right at us. I managed to shoot one, and Zinc plugged the other. They flopped over, twitching and shaking, and then one tried crawling towards us. I nailed him again. An-

102

other pair appeared—Dastrie got one of them, and the second was killed by Quent. I could hear multiple gunshots echoing somewhere down below as our hired help took care of business.

We kept to the cover provided by the main door to our office, methodically knocking the creatures down as they emerged from the elevator and stairwells.

"How many are there?" Dastrie yelled, catching yet another one on the fly.

"I'm hit," Jeff Jefferson screamed, as he slumped down the near wall, leaving a streak of blood.

"How bad?" I shouted over the din.

"Left arm: I'll be OK."

Then the firing abruptly stopped, and I cautiously eased myself out into the lobby. A dozen of the GNs were scattered here and there, all apparently dead. I could still hear a few shots being exchanged down below, but these gradually diminished as well.

I went back to Lizzie's desk and buzzed the front entrance. No response. Ditto the back door. Suddenly the bleat-bleat-bleat of a fire alarm jolted us out of our lethargy.

"Evacuate!" I yelled.

Zinc put one of his beefy arms under Jeff's shoulder, and got him to his feet. Everyone headed for the corner stairwell. I cracked open the door, and was greeted with a shot that caromed off the metal side. I returned fire, and heard a squeak from one of the gnomes.

I popped a new clip into my automatic, and fired several more covering shots down the stairs.

"Come on!" I ordered.

I could smell the smoke now. The little monsters must have fired the building when they realized they couldn't take it.

Step by step, I led the way down the three flights of stairs, occasionally exchanging gunfire with the remnants of the attacking gnomes. By the time we reached the first level, I could hear flames crackling not far away, and it was becoming difficult to breathe.

I pushed open the exit into the alleyway behind our building, and did a mental count to make certain that everyone on our floor had left. We were all coughing and choking by the time we found our way to the street out front. We were welcomed by the scream of sirens echoing in the distance.

I looked back.

Part of the bottom floor was now involved. Then I saw Moco. He was dangling out a window on the fourth floor. He hadn't reached the stairwell in time to evacuate.

Just then the first of the fire engines pulled up—a ladder truck—and they quickly unfurled the life-saving lattice. It was just long enough to rescue the cook, who was carried to safety before the smoke could overwhelm him.

Everyone else had been saved, except for three guards who'd been killed while fighting off the gnomes. Jeff was taken to the hospital by ambulance; they were afraid that the bone had been chipped in his upper left arm.

Twenty or thirty of the attackers had been killed or seriously wounded; the rest had withdrawn—but again, we found no bodies afterwards. Their companions must have carried them away.

The blaze itself was quickly brought under control by the Fire Department, but I could tell, even from the outside, that the building was heavily damaged by smoke and water. I had no idea how much we could salvage of our personal belongings.

"Oh, well, we'll just start over again," Dastrie finally said, her head coming to rest on my shoulder.

I put my arm around her and drew her close. She was the only damn thing worth saving out of the entire mess.

* * * * * * *

As I half expected, the gnomes also attacked Police Headquarters a few hours later, but Underhill and his men were waiting for them, and they killed a score or more of the little creatures before they withdrew.

"You should have seen us, Van," Fast Eddie said, when Dastrie and I joined him in his office. "They never knew what hit 'em!"

"Did you recover any of the bodies?" I asked.

I was curious why the gnomes had gone to such great efforts to keep us from examining their remains.

"Yes, indeedy, we've finally got some corpses of the creatures on ice down at the City Morgue—dunno how many. They're going to start dissectin' 'em this afternoon."

"I wonder if you could get permission for us to be present," I said.

He looked at me with an expression that stated, "You've got to be crazy."

"Sure, if that's what you really want," he finally said.

104

"Me too," Dastrie chimed in.

"Now wait just a moment," Underhill said. "That's no dang place for a lady."

She stared back at him, until finally her father finally shook his head and made a noise under his breath in exasperation: "All right, all right, I know when I'm beat. If that's what you really want...."

"I do, Daddy."

He picked up his phone, and asked his secretary to place the call to the Morgue.

Then I said: "That reminds me. I'd left a message yesterday for a friend of mine in Round Top to contact me at my office—which is obviously no longer possible. He doesn't have a phone himself, and I was wondering if I could use one of your lines to leave a message for him. I'll bill it to my account, of course."

When he agreed, I waltzed into the adjoining room to call the Round Toppian Dinette, which was located just a mile or so down the road from Willie Munn's hideaway near ShingleKill Falls. I explained the situation to Cherish LaPorte, the proprietress, and she said: "Oh, ya know, Willie Boy's here right now havin' hisself a plate o' them eels. Ya wanna talk to him?"

When I allowed as how I did, she nearly blasted out my eardrum with a shouted cry of "Willie Boy! Phone!"

"Yes, sir?" he finally said into the instrument. "Who the hell's this?"

"Richie Van Loan," I said. "Remember me from years past?"

"Van Loan? Oh, yes, sir. I 'member. Used to go fishin' with me up at the Falls."

"Great times we had too."

"Ah, yep!"

Willie Boy was not the most forthcoming of men, but he'd lived his entire life within a fifteen-mile radius of Round Top, and he knew everything there was to know about anyone and everyone who dwelt in the area. So I asked this local historian and gossip to bring me up-to-date on someone else we once knew together—and by gum and by golly, he 'membered just who I was talking 'bout too!

By the time I returned to Fast Eddie's office, the former Commissioner had obtained permission for Dastrie and me to visit the morgue.

"Find out what you wanted?" she asked me.

"I think so," I said.

When her father raised his eyebrows in question, I said, "Just a piece of personal history."

* * * * * * *

We took a cab to the Morgue, where we sought out Dr. W. L. Maltesius, one of the city medical examiners.

"Yes, I was told you were coming," he said, "although I don't know what business you amateurs have being here."

"Nevertheless," I said, "you talked to Mr. Underhill. If necessary, I can go further up the line."

"No reason to be huffy, sir," the M.E. said. "I already gave permission for you to observe the proceedings if you wish. We'll be starting in another ten minutes."

"Can we examine the bodies before they're dissected?" Dastrie asked.

"I suppose—but don't you dare touch anything! Katherine!" he yelled at someone in the other room. When the stern-faced attendant in her sixties appeared, he said: "These, uh, people want to view the bodies of the Nasty Gnomes."

"*What*, sir?" she said.

"They have my leave," Maltesius said.

"Very well, sir. Follow me, folks."

She led us down a corridor, and abruptly turned into a cold room where the recently deceased were laid out on stretchers. The GNs looked almost like children under the sheets, their short bodies completely shrouded in white.

"Would you peel back the coverings, please?" I said.

Katherine frowned at the imposition, but went over to the first corpse and rolled back the linen.

"Now, that's strange!" she said.

"What?" Dastrie asked.

"Well, I was told that these, uh, things were pretty badly shot up. But this one is completely free of wounds."

She rushed over to an adjoining body. "And this one too."

"Let me see," I said—and sure enough, the corpses were unmarked, other than blood stains. There were signs that injuries had once been inflicted, but none of the entrance or exit holes were now evident.

Then something stirred right behind us. We turned around, and watched as one of the bodies that was still enshrouded gradually sat up, the sheet slowly sliding down its face. Its eyes snapped open, and the head rotated to fix us with its gaze.

"Saint Camber!" the attendant screamed, and ran out of the room.

Then the other stiffs began unstiffening, one by one, and Dastrie whispered, "You know, Richard, I think we might want to get out of here."

But by the time we headed towards the door, it was already blocked by one of the creatures.

"One-Eye sends his regards," the little man hissed, before turning and bolting out the exit.

His compatriots quickly followed suit, all except one.

"Be careful!" Dastrie shouted, when I approached the last of the covered bodies. I carefully slid the covering away from its face. There was a bullet hole pocked right between its ugly yellow eyes.

I reached out and touched its skin, and then quickly withdrew my hand: it was ice cold and almost slimy, with a damp sheen that shouldn't have been there in that arid environment. I went over to the sink and thoroughly washed myself.

Suddenly Dr. Maltesius appeared in the doorway.

"What's going on here? What have you done with my gnomes?"

"They just got up and walked away," Dastrie said. "All except this one!"

"That's impossible. They were certified as deceased by the ambulance techs, and checked by me when they first arrived here. They had no pulses or respiration or other signs of life."

"Nonetheless," I said, "they revived. But this one"—I pointed to my little buddy lying prone on the table—"He seems to have suffered a fatal injury when he was shot in the head."

"I just don't understand this," the M.E. said. "There should have been no way that any of these, uh, things could possibly have come to life again. They were dead, I tell you, dead as dead can be."

"Well, they're not dead now. However, you still have one body left to dissect."

"Harrumph!" (He actually said that, the first time in my memory that I'd ever heard the expression.)

Then he ordered the gnome rolled into the examination room, and got started with his slicing and dicing.

By the time he was done, two and one half hours later, I'd paid homage to the toilet bowl god at least twice, while Dastrie just stood there stoically, quite unaffected by all the carnage. It's one thing to experience death on the battlefield or in a back alley somewhere; it's quite another to see a man's corpus calmly taken apart piece by gory piece.

"So what's the verdict, Doc?" I asked.

"Don't call me 'Doc'," came the reply. "My name is Dr. Maltesius. He died of a gunshot wound to the brain."

"I could have told you that."

"Yes, but there's something wrong with his blood. I'll have to have it analyzed to be sure, but it just, well, smells funny."

"Is that a medical term?" I asked.

He gave me a dirty look and frowned.

"Come over here and I'll show you," the M.E. said.

I edged very slowly and carefully to the metal table, trying to salvage what little I had left of breakfast. Then I noticed it: a kind of musty odor, like mushrooms in an autumn rain.

"See what I mean?"

"Some kind of drug?" I asked.

"Maybe. But the coagulated blood doesn't look right either. It's lighter in color than it should be. And the body is misshapen—I mean, more than normal for a dwarf. The muscular structure is enhanced beyond anything that should be possible with exercise. Also, I found another wound down on the creature's left leg—it's half healed, even though it's obvious that the bullet to the head killed the gnome almost instantly."

"Do you think the injuries happened simultaneously?"

"No. My guess is that the thigh wound occurred some hours or days before the other. But how could it heal so quickly?"

"Anything else?"

"The skin seemed damp to me—but that's also very odd. I'm going to have to do a series of tests, and probably call in some experts; but even then, I doubt if I'm going to be able to provide many more answers. This is way beyond anything I've experienced—and I've viewed hundreds of corpses over the years."

"Thank you, Doctor."

I was edging back towards the door again, trying to keep my queasy stomach in check.

"These experiments are grotesque," my wife said, as we entered a cab. "They've obviously affected these poor people in ways that may not be retrievable."

"Our only hope is that removing them from the source of the drug, whatever it is, will cure and not kill them," I said.

Dastrie smiled sweetly at me.

"Care for an early dinner, Richard?" she asked. "Italian?"

I belched out loud. "Oh, give it a rest!" I said.

I couldn't have eaten anything then if I'd been starving to death.

* * * * * * *

I rented an entire floor—the penthouse—of the Grand Marnier Hotel facing on Central Park (I owned a share of the place), and arranged that dinner be served in our suite for the members of our crew. Access to the top floor was restricted to a locked elevator opening onto a small, separate lobby, and I made sure that a contingent of armed guards was permanently posted there.

When most of our people—including the long-absent Sergeant Castelluccio, but lacking Jeff Jefferson, who was still hospitalized—had appeared, I toasted their courage and steadfastness, and promised them a share of the monies we'd secured through the previous day's efforts.

"Obviously, we'll rebuild," I said, while dessert—a *crème brûlée*—was being served, "together with your help, and with much time and effort. I want to reconstruct a headquarters that's secure for the future—either here or elsewhere, if we can agree on a site that's better positioned for us. We'll discuss the matter further at a later date.

"However, we still have our primary task at hand: eliminating the threat of the Nasty Gnomes. This has to be our number one goal so long as they still pose a threat to society. We obviously need to coordinate our efforts with the police, National Guard, and other security forces currently operating in the city—and former Commissioner Underhill will help to facilitate this.

"I intend to make one last visit to Rotary headquarters in Harlem tomorrow morning to see if there's any way we can resolve the crisis through negotiations. If we can't, then we need to focus our efforts on an all-out assault on what I believe to be the gnomes' center of operations—the Fraternal Rotary of Gnomes building and whatever lies below it.

"Since it's difficult to kill the gnomes, we need to capture as many as possible, and secure them in some safe location until we see if they can be weaned from their drug, whatever that is. If severing them from their supply of the chemical ultimately kills them, then so be it. Either way the problem will be solved.

"The larger question of who's responsible for the development of the experimental serum may have to be left to a later date.

"Any questions?"

"How can we help?" Franky Castelluccio asked.

"I want all of you here promptly at one o'clock tomorrow afternoon," I said. "Then I'll give you my final instructions for the day. Sergeant, I know you have other duties to attend to until the emergency has passed; just let us know, please, where you can be reached. Lizzie will be present here all day tomorrow to act as coordinator of our communications net."

Then I dismissed them to their homes.

About an hour later, I was buzzed by the main desk.

"A gentleman to see you, sir," the concierge said.

"What's his name?"

"A Mr. R. M. Cohn."

I sighed and nodded at Dastrie, who nodded back.

"Send him up!" I ordered.

A few minutes later there was a knock on the main entrance to the penthouse, and I opened the door, motioning the attorney to enter. He was clothed all in gray, with a nondescript tie of some beige color, and an overcoat and hat to mitigate the chill outside.

"Mr. Van Loan," he said, holding out his hand, "We meet again."

I ignored his fist and introduced Dastrie.

"And what brings you to our temporary home away from home?" I asked.

"First, my regret over the attack on your building. The times we live in are perilous ones indeed."

"I can tell that you're all broken up about it," I said. "In point of fact, we actually live out on Long Island, as you well know. My office is just another way station in which to rest our feet along the way."

"Well, I did warn you to be careful about the choices you make," the attorney said. "You're either for us or against us."

"Who's us?" Dastrie asked.

"The right-thinking people, the men and women fighting for the values that America should—and must—support. We're involved in a war for the very spirit of this great country, a war that we can't possibly afford to lose. The enemy is an implacable foe who will never abandon the fight, and who will do anything in his power to subvert the population to his cause. I fear that you may be coming gradually under his influence."

"Are you saying that the Nasty Gnomes are creatures of the Communists and Socialists?" I asked.

"That might well be true, but how would I know, really?"

"They do seem to be associated in some fashion with The Organization Against the Defamation of Little People—and I believe you have a relationship with that foundation, don't you?"

"I'm their lawyer, as is stated on their letterhead."

"I thought you were a member of their Board of Directors."

"Actually, Mr. Van Loan, I'm not, as the Chairman of the Board can confirm. And my dealings with that organization clearly fall under the principle of client-attorney privilege, and thus are not subject to questioning by any other authority.

"Furthermore, I've decided to sever my relationship with that group, effective immediately."

"But didn't you arrange for certain individuals to make significant financial contributions in support of the foundation?"

"Again, what I may or may not have facilitated for other clients is not subject to discussion here—and in any case, lies clearly within the letter of the law."

"Then why *are* you here, Mr. Cohn?"

"Mr. Van Loan, you've damaged the interests of certain individuals whom I represent, and they've asked me to pass along a message to you."

"Which is?"

"'What's done is done. Keep what you've stolen, and nothing more will be said about it. However, cross us again and the most drastic steps will be taken against you and yours.'

"I know these people, Mr. Van Loan. They don't make idle threats. They represent some of the wealthiest, most influential, most powerful men of our generation. What they say will happen, will in fact happen; and neither you nor anyone else can stop them from achieving whatever they wish to do. They have almost infinite resources.

"As a kind of *bona fide*, they asked me to give you this."

He handed me a page from the late edition of *The New York Informer*, with a story outlined in red ink on page sixteen:

FOUL FLUSH IN RIO!

RIO DE JANEIRO, AP, Dec. 23. Brazilian police report the discovery of the body of a murdered man in a locked restroom cubicle at the Rio de Janeiro Airport, his head stuffed into the toilet. The man has been tentatively identified as New York accountant, Raúl Luis Villa Mendosa, age 46. He had apparently flown

THE NASTY GNOMES, BY ROBERT REGINALD

there from New York City earlier in the day. The motive for his killing was apparently robbery. Anyone having information on the case should contact Capitão João Braganza of the Rio de Janeiro Police Dept.

"Is this supposed to scare me?" I asked, passing the page to Dastrie.

"No, Mr. Van Loan, it's supposed to make you think! I also have a personal message for you."

"And that is?"

He reached inside his bulky coat, pulled out an envelope, and handed it to me. I slit open the flap with a penknife. It was a summons to appear a month hence before the Senate Permanent Subcommittee on Investigations.

"We want to know about your association with known Communists, Mr. Van Loan. I've been looking into your background, and have discovered some very disturbing information about your activities over the past thirty years. I think you're a very dangerous man, and I'm sure the American public will be very much interested to know all of the details as they're revealed in our hearings."

"I thought Senator McCarthy already had enough troubles piled on his plate with Edward R. Murrow exposing his slipshod relationship to the truth."

"We'll see, Mr. Van Loan, we'll see. I don't think Mr. Murrow has ever encountered anyone quite like you! Of course, I can make this all go away, if...."

"If I agree to cooperate with you?"

"Something like that."

"I don't think so, Mr. Cohn," I said. "You're a bully, and so's your boss; and bullies can only be dealt with one way: by facing them down. If you think you have damaging information about me, by all means bring it front and center, and we'll see who survives the confrontation. You don't want me as an enemy."

"The same could be said of me," Cohn replied.

"Then may the best man win," I said. "And now I think I've had quite enough of you for one evening. It's time for you to go away, to retreat back into that deep, dark den where you dwell—you and your vicious little secrets. And I know you must have some of your own hidden away that you don't want revealed. You can count on me to find them, sir—each and every one!"

Then he gave me a look of absolute vitriol, a glimpse into the vileness of his soul, and headed for the exit. Just before he closed the door, he stared back at me and said: "Do keep an eye on that lovely wife of yours, Mr. Van Loan. You wouldn't want her to stray too far from safety—now, would you?"

Before I could do anything to stop her, Dastrie reached into her purse and pulled out her little .22. She waved it at him.

"Anyone who tries fooling around with me will have to reckon with my little friend here. Several of those who've done so in the past are now dead."

Then she very deliberately shot a hole through the attorney's hat, knocking it off his head.

He ran out into the lobby, slamming the door behind him.

"You OK, sir," one of the guards barked over the intercom.

"We're fine," I replied.

Then I just started laughing.

"Gee, I can't take you anywhere, can I?" I said to my wife.

She flipped the safety on and stuffed the gun back into her bag.

"Let's go listen to *The Shadow* on the radio; it'll be coming on soon. I just love the old pulp serials."

"Yes, they'll all be gone before too much longer, just like me. Television's replacing the great shows of yesteryear."

She warmed up the console, and we both listened to that eerie introduction: "'Who knows what evil lurks in the hearts of men? The Shadow knows!'"

* * * * * * *

Much later that night, when Dastrie slept safely and securely and serenely within Slumberland, I slipped out of our bed and tip-toed into the next room. There I quietly dressed myself all in black, complete with coat and hat, and gently departed the suite, motioning to the guards to keep quiet.

Down in the lobby of the hotel, I dropped a coin into one of the pay phones, and dialed a number. It rang several times before I got a gruff "Yeah!" barked back at me from the other end of the line.

"Two-eleven-nineteen-zero," I said in response. "Hotel Grand Marnier, fifteen minutes."

Then I hung up the receiver, and sat down with a stray copy of the *Times*, perusing the obits.

A quarter of an hour later I walked out the front door to the street, and stepped up to a black sedan that rolled to a stop in front of me. I opened its right rear door and got in.

"The Four Elephants in Brooklyn," I said, as I settled back onto the plush leather seat.

There was no response from the driver, but the automobile smoothly accelerated down the street. I flipped open a console in front of me, and calmly removed two automatics and several extra slips, stuffing them down inside the pockets of my dark overcoat—together with the silk ebon mask, of course.

Earlier in the day, I'd cornered Belle Darling and asked her where I could find the ventriloquist, Justus Goebel. I had something I needed to ask him, and he was going to provide me with an answer, one way or the other.

It took us forty-five minutes to reach the bar in Brooklyn that Mr. Goebel frequented. I slipped on the guise of my alter-ego and stepped out of the car a block distant, at a point where I could unobtrusively observe the main entrance. The sedan purred on down the street; it would return at regular intervals through the night.

And then I waited.

I loved the night. I loved the sights and sounds and smells and creatures—human and animal—that roamed through the dark. I let my senses expand outward, following the discipline that I'd been taught in Bhutan several decades earlier, and I felt and savored and heard everything that happened within the range of my vision—a range more encompassing by far than most.

My mechanical courier passed me by at fifteen-minute intervals. I ignored it. My attention was focused solely on the garish neon sign displaying four pink elephants prancing up and down over the main entrance of the place. Patrons entered and patrons left, but I was looking for a specific individual—a man with one eye.

Finally Goebel himself appeared in the doorway, staggering under the cumulated weight of several decades' worth of empty bottles. I could hear him singing some dirty ditty under his breath—

> "I once knew a gal named Gidget,
> Whose boobs had plenty of fidget;
> When she played the papoose,
> All hell would break loose,
> Her billows would swallow the midget."

I eased myself from shadow to shadow and doorway to doorway as I tailed him down the darkened streets of Brooklyn, stalking my prey in the age-old chase of hunter and hunted.

Gad, it was great to be back on the streets again.

The darkness enfolded me in her lusty embrace, and I could feel my heart pumping and my blood flowing as I silently glided down the seedy byways of the city. For such a drunken man, Goebel was surprisingly agile, and seemed to be headed for a specific destination.

Finally, he paused in front of a small house, pulled out a key, and fumbled at the door, trying to get it open.

Then I pounced!

"Wh-what?" he blathered, as he tried to figure out what was happening to him.

I pulled him into a black hollow under a bush, covering his mouth with my gloved hand.

"Tell me about Petite Souris," I ordered the man, unstopping his mouth.

"No!" was the gut response. "He-he's crazy!"

"Tell me about Petite Souris," I repeated, bending one of his arms back until it began to hurt.

"I-I can't! He-he'll kill me!"

"Tell me about Petite Souris!" I demanded, "Or *I* will kill you here and now!"

"Ahhh!" he gasped out in pain. "S-stop. OK. I-I'll tell you."

"Tell me about Petite Souris!"

"He came back and put out my eye," the ventriloquist said, almost crying. "He and his friends: they put out my eye!"

"Why?"

"Be-because I knew too much about him, he said—he said—he said—he said…." Then he hiccupped.

I shook him hard. "Snap out of it!"

"He-he said that if I told, he would take the other eye as well."

"Told *what?*"

"Oh, oh God, I can't say."

I bent his arm back even further.

"St-stop! Please! Once, when we got drunk together, he told me his life story, told me how his family was ruined. And he said he only lived now to get revenge on the Big People. All of the Big People. And on one Big Person in particular."

Suddenly the front door cracked opened and a bright light slashed across the front porch.

"Justy? Is that you?" a woman's squeaky voice asked.

Before I could do anything, the ventriloquist twisted out of my grasp and ran for safety. I just caught a glimpse of a three-foot-high figure silhouetted in the doorway, before the aperture slammed shut in my face.

I didn't try to pursue him further. I'd found what I wanted.

I made my way slowly back to the street, back to the point where I'd been dropped off several hours earlier.

Five minutes later, the black sedan oozed out of the night and poured itself on the street in front of me. I pried open the right rear door, and settled myself down on the leather seat, while peeling off my mask.

"The Grand Marnier," I said, to no one in particular, and the automobile accelerated once more, taking me back to my refuge.

Oh, I so loved the silky embrace of the night.

To roam the night.

To spread the night.

To *be* the night.

And Zero at the Bone.

CHAPTER ELEVEN

HICKORY DICKORY DOCK
▲
Hickory dickory dock,
The mouse ran up the clock,
The clock struck one,
The mouse ran down,
Hickory dickory dock.

—Traditional verse
▼
New York, New York
Thursday, 24 December 1953

If Dastrie was aware of my absence the previous evening, she said nothing about it the next morning. My sweet wife had her own demons to tame, and knew that there were times when the wild things had to be let loose from their cage in order to allow the veneer of civilization to be sustained.

"Did you sleep well?" she asked, carefully sipping her coffee across from me.

"Oh, deeply, furiously, indisputably," I countered.

"So I can see. What's on the agenda today?"

"Another pass at the FROGgies, I think. We need to determine if they're eating flies or humming humbugs or whatever these days. I would prefer to end this case bloodlessly, but end it we will."

"It would be nice to celebrate Christmas together in peace," she said, slipping a bit of toast slathered with red currants between those perfect white teeth.

"Crunch," they went, "crunch, crunch, crunch."

I could have watched them masticate all day long, oh yes!

Did I tell you that we were perfectly matched?

However, it was time to be about our brothers' business, and so I rang the bell to clear the table—in more ways than one. I took a supremely hot-and-cold shower, and dressed warmly for our excursion.

It was cold out there in Harlem.

The headquarters of the Fraternal Rotary of Gnomes was just as inviting as before: a clean building, a well-maintained building, a building shrouded and sheathed and spiked with icicles, frozen in a state not unlike grace. I distrusted such appearances instinctively.

The same miniature receptionist greeted us behind her hole-in-the-wall alcove.

"Yes?"

"You remember us," I said. "We were here last Friday."

"You BPs all look alike to me."

She smiled. With her crooked teeth, it wasn't her most attractive feature.

"We'd like to see Mr. Smith again," Dastrie said.

"He's very busy today."

"Busy? It's Christmas Eve, Miss…?"

"It's Miss Smith," she said. "And to answer your question, *that's* why he's busy. So many festivities and all." She pointed to the miniature tree that had been erected in the far corner: a porcelain gnome crowned the very top, drooping down towards the floor.

"Any relation to Mr. Smith?"

"Yes. We're both Little People."

"We'd still like to talk to him."

She tweaked the com button, and when it buzzed, said: "Mr. Smith, there's a couple of BPs to see you."

He said something that I couldn't hear, and she looked at me.

"Your names?"

"Richard Curtis Van Loan and Dastrie Lee Van Loan."

She repeated this into the instrument, and a blather-blather-blather rattled back at her.

"Fine. Go on in. You apparently know the way." She tilted her head back at the rear door.

Alexander Smith was as comfy as ever behind his plush oak desk, well upholstered in his angora sweater, puffing on a cheroot that had the aroma of Fulgencio Batista about it.

"Third time's a charm, Mr. Van Loan—or so they say." He bowed his head at Dastrie. "Madame, a pleasure to see you again, I'm sure. What brings you both to the haunts of Harlem?"

"Nothing but yourself," I said, "and a desire to end the bloodshed that's permeating our two communities."

"What a laudable sentiment! Who could oppose such aims? Who could possibly benefit from continued strife?" He huffed and he puffed some more, stretching his purple lips around the butt of that big brown cigar.

"You know, that's just what I was wondering. '*Cui bono?*' as Cicero once said. And it occurred to me, Mr. Smith, that *you* might benefit, in a perverse sort of way."

He pulled his stogie out of his mouth and pointed it at me. A trail of smoke wound its way towards the ceiling, lassoing the vitriol that came pouring out of the black hole thereby left vacant: "Why, that's a despicable notion! Absolutely dastardly, sir! How dare you!"

"I dare because I know things about you, Mr. Smith, that the rest of the world doesn't know—but soon will. I know, for example, that you were once Petite Souris, the dummy comedian."

"I worked as a performer, yes," he admitted, "but everyone in the business knows that. Making fools out of ourselves is about the only way we Little People can earn an honest living, Mr. Van Loan. The world so despises us that it leaves us no option but to endure the jibes and japes of an uncaring audience.

"Finally I reached a point where I could live with the shame no longer. My own despite at constantly playing the fool forced me to redefine myself at last, to see myself for the man that I am. The words that the ventriloquist put into my mouth—or so the crowd thought—were *my* words in actuality, and they weren't really funny, not to me. In the end, they weren't very funny to that drunken sot, either."

"So you took his eye."

"'If thine eye offend thee, pluck it out!'"

"Is that where you got the name One-Eye?"

"To paraphrase Ogden Nash: the one-eyed lama, he's a priest; the two-eyed llama, he's a beast; and I will bet a silk pajama, there's no such thing as a three-eyed lllama."

"All of these pseudonyms: why do you so love hiding behind them?" I asked.

"Why do you hide behind *your* mask?" he countered. "You accuse me of…whatever, and yet you don't hesitate to shoot down our people if they get in your way. You show no more mercy for them than you would a fly on the wall."

"They can't help what they've become," I said, "but they're still a danger to innocent men, women, and children."

"None of you Big People are innocent. Not really. You've connived to place us in servitude, to make us a mockery of a caricature of a buffoonery. It's not your hate that I despise, it's your contempt. Whatever I've done here is nothing in comparison with your constant condemnation of our humanity."

"That may be so," I acknowledged, "but it doesn't really change things in the end, Mr. Smith. Because this is *not* about the rights or the needs or the importance of the Little People: it's about you and me, isn't it? It's about the sins of our fathers, Mr. Maussey."

His dark eyes overflowed with anger, and for a moment the hate clogged even his vocal cords. He made his smoke-stick his weapon of choice again.

"You...*you* killed him, Van Loan!" was all he was finally able to blurt out.

"Did I?" I said.

"It took me years to find out what had happened to my father. My mother remarried Jeffrey Smith, and would tell me nothing about my Dad, only that he was a good-for-nothing asshole that had left us penniless."

"But that wasn't true."

"It *was* true. He was ashamed of me, and he left his estate to the three children by his first wife, saying that my mother had had an affair with another man, and that I was not his son, even though I bore his name. My mother went to court to challenge the will, but my half-brother brought forth an affidavit saying that the allegations were valid; and because my father had divorced my mother a few months before his death, she was only allowed the pittance that she'd received under the settlement.

"Still, I wanted to know how my father had died—for there was no doubt in my mind that I *was* his son. Peter Maussey Sr. had been murdered, but the police had dropped the case for lack of evidence. I could find little on my own, however.

"And then one night, when I was playing that stupid little dummy up there on the stage, that idiot drunk farted so loud that everyone heard; and in the brief silence that followed, I heard a voice whispering from the front row, ever so quietly, 'I know who killed your Dad.' I walked off the stage and never came back."

"And that was when you met him," I said.

"I never knew his name, and he never revealed his face to me, not directly. He said, 'Call me Smith.'

"I told him, 'That's *my* name!'"

"He said, 'So it is. I think we're all Smiths in this world. You want something from me, Mr. Smith, and I want something from you. That sounds like a good arrangement for me—and a very profitable one for you. And it'll help your people as well.'

"And so I followed him. He was as good as his word. He paid me a great deal of money, he helped my people, and he gave me, in the end—he gave me *your* name, Mr. Van Loan."

"But he never told you why," I said. "And the context, my dear Mr. Smith, is everything. I'm so sorry you've been used and abused, and not in a very nice way; but what you've done has caused more harm to the Little People than anything they've endured from us over the centuries."

"That's a lie!"

"No, it isn't!" I said. "But I do think that your little tale is mostly sound and fury, signifying nothing. You see, I saw you talking with Cohn at Santy's Village. You two were clearly well acquainted. So he isn't your mystery man, as you would have me think.

"In point of fact, he's just a conduit for the money. He happens to be connected to rich and powerful individuals who want something from the foundation—and you used *him*, not the other way 'round. Although I wouldn't be surprised, in the end, if he doesn't find a way to screw your 'little' group as well. He seems to be very good at that sort of thing. Not a nice man to know well.

"But you're not very nice either. You haven't been completely honest with us, Mr. Smith. The incident with Farticus the ventriloquist was correct, insofar as the 'blowout' you described; but there was no one whispering sweet nothings from the audience, just you walking out on a fellow performer. And that occurred in the mid-1940s, not recently, as you would have us believe.

"And then you and your bully-boys terrorized him, and that was great fun, wasn't it? Suddenly your fidgety midgety complex didn't seem quite so small after all. You could give as good as you got. Goebel wasn't going to say anything about your precious past—he couldn't even remember most of what you'd told him.

"The truth is, you hated your Dad! It's the age-old story: the son treads upon the footsteps of the father and can't measure up, and so he has to take it out on the weak and powerless.

"And as for me supposedly killing your father…. You picked my name out of a long list of possible assassins, only because I was wealthier than the rest. You have no evidence, no witnesses, nothing to tie me to the crime. You just wanted to extort money from me. Well, you won't get a two-penny piece!

"But this still doesn't tell us what you were doing, Mr. Smith, between 1945 and 1950, when you became Director of this facility."

He smiled then, a queer little crab of a thing that threatened to crawl right off his face. I realized at that moment that he was quite, even superbly insane.

"You ever read *The Strange Case of Dr. Jekyll and Mr. Hyde,* Mr. Van Loan? I loved that story as a kid. A man who was nothing suddenly became SOMEBODY, just by drinking a potion. He might have been a monster, but he was a monster that everyone feared and respected.

"I tried to find another way of making a living, I really did, but in 1945 and '46 the streets were flooded with returning servicemen, and no one would hire me. Why should they, when there were so many able-bodied, true-blue Americans looking for work? Not even the shelters wanted me. I think I reminded them too much of Ole Nibs. They'd toss me some scraps, and then boot me right out.

"One day I overheard a couple of bums talking outside one of the missions.

"'Don't do it!' the first one said.

"'I need a drink real bad, Fred,' the second one responded.

"I finally realized, after listening to them for an hour, that someone out there was willing to give this trash some hard money for serving as guinea pigs for a new tonic. I would have died and gone to heaven to've had two bucks in my pocket right about then.

"'That stuff makes you feel all oogie inside,' Fred said.

"'I gotta have the money,' number two bum replied.

"And then the first one told the second where he could find the guy—in Harlem. But I got there first!

"The man's name was Rollini.

"'*Dr.* Rollini,' he said.

"He looked me up and down, and said, 'We haven't had one of *your* kind before. This should be very interesting.'

"'Three bucks,' I replied."

Then Smith cocked his oversized head at me and laughed—a high, chickeny kind of cackle. It gave me the chilly-willies.

"He paid it too," the little man finally said, when he'd controlled himself. "And again! And again! Finally, Rollini told me he wanted a long-term relationship. And so I became his 'minimacaroni,' as he was fond of calling me—the primary test subject for his 'Energizer.'

"He'd started working on a government contract during the war. He was supposed to develop a formula that'd boost the performance of tired soldiers, something to eliminate their fatigue and battle weariness. When the conflict ended in 1945, Washington forgot to terminate the agreement, and he continued receiving checks for his research. Once or twice a year he'd send reports to a P.O. Box in Laurel, Maryland—but he never received a response.

"So he just continued working on his stuff, using skid row denizens as his test subjects—and then me, when I came along.

"I have no idea what was in the goop. It tasted a little different each time, as he tried varying the ingredients and the dosages. Sometimes I'd get sick from even a sip, sometimes I'd feel exhilarated, sometimes I'd be depressed, sometimes I'd break out in hives. But I finally had something to do, something for which I was being well paid, something that was even patriotic in its way. I have no doubt he was a genius. He was absolutely obsessed with the thing.

"And then one day he gave me Formula #666. It had a nutty aroma about it, not unpleasant, and when I drank the glass down, I felt no immediate aftereffect. It was just another witch's brew, so far as I was concerned.

"But the next morning, I had trouble pulling my pants on. You have to understand, Mr. Van Loan, that our clothes are individually tailored. You can't buy them in stores. They're fitted to us personally.

"When I reported this phenomenon to Dr. Rollini, he became highly agitated.

"'How do you feel otherwise?' he asked.

"I said I felt really good, even great—and the truth was, I'd never felt better in my life. I was full of vim and vigor, yin and yang: I could do anything! The Energizer was working!

"Over a period of months, we tried various parameters with the drug. Discontinuing it, even for brief periods, would result in me gradually reverting to my former height and weight. But maintaining the dosage caused certain side effects.

"My face started puffing out, my muscles began developing to an extraordinary degree, and my emotions began jumping up and down almost beyond my ability to control them. I became remarkably susceptible to suggestion, to the point where I could be made to do almost anything by the command of my 'control'—in this case, Rollini.

"It was amusing at first, but I soon came to see Rollini in the same light that I'd once viewed Goebel—he was using me for his own ends, like all the BPs, and he cared nothing about me personally. But as long as I was taking the Energizer, my will was mere putty in his sculptor's hands.

"Then Rollini made a mistake: he filed another report with his invisible overseers in Laurel, Maryland, telling them of his great success. After who knows how many years of experimenting with the damned drug, he'd finally found something—and he just couldn't resist telling 'Them' about it! He had to boast!

"Well, 'Them' responded.

"By this time I'd gained six inches in height, seemingly the maximum possible with this particular formula, together with enormous new strength in my torso and arms. When I reported to 'work' a few days later, Dr. Rollini was arguing with someone.

"'But it's *my* research,' he said. '*I* developed it.'

"'And we paid for it,' the other man replied. 'You've made a breakthrough, Rollini, no question, but it's time for us to transfer this project to a fully funded and staffed research laboratory. You can be part of that effort, if you wish—indeed, we desperately *want* your participation—but someone else will actually have to administer all future research and development from now on. Sorry, but that's the way it's got to be.'

"'No, I can't allow this,' Rollini repeated. 'It's *mine!*'

"'Not any longer,' the official said, and started to pick up the doctor's telephone.

"'Stop him!' my master ordered, and I couldn't refuse.

"I picked up a small granite paperweight from Rollini's desk, and threw it across the room—at least fifteen feet—hitting the fed right on the back of his head. He fell to the floor with a thud. I knew immediately he was dead.

"'What are we going to do?' Rollini asked, looking on the verge of a breakdown. 'Why did you have to kill him?'

"'You told me to stop him,' I said.

"'Shit, shit, shit!' Then he rattled something off in Italian. 'Tell me what to do, you little twerp!'

"He was almost like a child when he wasn't working on his research.

"'Are you ordering me to take charge?' I asked.

"'Yes, yes, yes, isn't that what I said?'"

"'Very well, we have to leave this place immediately. I'll find a new place for us to work, and make arrangements to relocate everything there. Meanwhile, I want you to sit down over here at your desk, and start purging your paperwork. You should burn everything not related to the Energizer—and begin writing a detailed account of how to generate the formula, step by step, with a list of the specific chemicals and equipment required to do so. All the rest must go.'

"I knew quite a few LPs who were out of work, just like me before I'd encountered Rollini—and they weren't very particular about what they did. I made some calls, and I soon had a crew of twenty reliable men to assist me—with the promise that they too would be given doses of the formula to increase their height and strength.

"They disposed of the body somewhere underground—I don't know where, and it's never been found. The apparatus and supplies were moved to an old warehouse in Harlem. We burned the original lab that evening. When we set up the new facility, Dr. Rollini continued working on enhancements to his drug—while I gradually weaned myself off of it.

"The good doctor didn't know that our shoes had switched feet—he'd done it himself when he'd ordered me to take control. I continued to play the fool, a role that I had long perfected, and when the time came, Rollini joined his friend in the New York underground.

"That was 1950, wasn't it?" I said.

"Yes. I was able to engineer my appointment as the new Director of the Rotary by promising the LPs doses of my drug—and it *was* mine now, in every sense of the word. As each of the Little People became hooked on the formula, they became, quite literally, *my* creatures."

"And the government never found you?"

"Ah. We eventually came to another arrangement," the little man said.

"Of course! Cohn!" Dastrie suddenly exclaimed.

"Yes, Mr. Cohn was the key. He was quite approachable, actually, and he had all the connections, in and out of the government, to funnel significant amounts of cash into our project."

"And what did *he* want from you?" I asked. "He's not the kind of man to work without a *quid pro quo*."

"Oh, they all want the formula, of course," Smith said. "It would perhaps give them an edge in certain other arenas. But they don't have it yet—and they never will—just a few samples that I've provided them. I'm the only one who knows the recipe, and no one else will ever get it."

"Mr. Cohn isn't likely to accept such an arrangement permanently."

"Of course not," the LP said. "But he has much to lose if his connection with this project ever became known—so does his boss, Senator McCarthy. I don't know specifically why they wanted the Energizer, but it doesn't matter, really. They won't get it, not from me—and there's nothing they can do to force me to give it to them. Any more than you can force me to do what *you* want, Mr. Van Loan."

"Why did you kill Roscoe?" I asked.

"He was involved with Ruby Diamond. She used him to spy on the Rotary Building for that stupid brother of hers, and before we realized what Mr. Wallace was up to, he discovered several examples of our, well, less successful subjects. He had to be removed before he could tell anyone—in this case you, whenever you returned from California.

"I questioned him myself, and when I realized exactly who his employer was, I thought it would be the perfect chance to finish the work my father had begun. And if you *had* been involved in my Dad's death, then justice would be served.

"Now, of course, none of that matters. You've satisfied my purpose, and I no longer care what happens to either one of you."

Dastrie abruptly pulled her shiny little .22 from her purse, and leveled it right at the Director's face. "If you're dead, you won't be a threat to anyone," she said.

"Go ahead, pull the trigger! You won't live to leave this room. The building is wired with explosives. My followers will blow the place before allowing themselves to be captured. And after I'm gone, someone else will take my position. I've made plans, you see."

"Maybe I don't believe you," my wife said, "and maybe I don't care in any case. You kidnapped my father!"

"And I returned him when the ransom was paid," Smith said. "I'm a man of my word."

"You're a bald-faced liar, Smith or Maussey or Souris," I interjected. "We've already established that."

There was a slight click as Dastrie flipped off the safety of her automatic.

"Wait!" the little man said. "Just a moment!"

"Keep your hands out where I can see them," I said. "Stand up!"

His fingers were moving up and down on the surface of his desk as he pushed his leather chair back. Suddenly he smiled again.

"Be seeing you!" he said.

And then he just disappeared!

The bang of Dastrie's gun echoed throughout the room—but she was too late! The back wall of the office sprouted a pimple.

"Damn it!" she shouted, rushing over to the other side of the Director's desk. "Look at *this*, Richard!"

I saw a round hole in the floor next to the chair, and beneath it a metal tube of some sort that petered away into the darkness. Even as I watched, the hatch silently slid shut.

A siren abruptly began hooting, two shorts and a long, and we looked at each other.

"Maybe we better get out of here," I said.

We ran back into the receptionist's area, but Miss Smith was gone—and, in fact, we didn't see anyone else as we headed out the main entrance. The door slowly swung shut behind us, and we could hear it latch itself.

The sound of the warning signal became more intense, the beeps occurring at shorter intervals. We carefully backed away from the structure, as the occupants of the neighboring buildings began crowding into the street to see what was happening.

And then it began.

Cracks appeared in the façade of the masonry, and inched their way up the side of the structure, growing wider even as we watched. When they reached the top floor, pieces of the exterior began flaking off, scattering the groups of onlookers. Then whole chunks of the walls began collapsing, and finally the rest of the building folded in upon itself, shaking the very ground as it became an immense garbage heap of broken bricks and broken dreams.

The FROGgies had finally croaked!

* * * * * * *

"What the hell did you think you were doing, Van?" Fast Eddie Underhill yelled.

"We were trying to save the city from further bloodshed," Dastrie said, attempting to mollify her father. "And I think we did a pretty good job of it, too."

"You do, huh?" the former Police Commissioner said. "Then where *are* they, Dastrie? We found a dozen bodies of the gnomes in the wreckage itself—and Smith's isn't among them. We did locate some mangled pieces of lab equipment and some ruptured containers of the drug, but nothin' else that might lead us to the ringleaders. So where have they gone?"

"They were already planning to shut down their Harlem operation by Christmas Day," I said.

"So?"

We looked at each other for another few minutes, and then I finally had to admit defeat.

"I don't know," I said. "I just don't know."

"Oh, get the hell out of here, both of you," Underhill said, motioning us towards the door of his office. "The Mayor has already declared our operation a success, and I just hope to God he's right this time—and you better hope so too, Mr. and Mrs. Van Loan, you better damn well hope so too!"

We went back to the Grand Marnier, our tails tucked very carefully between our legs.

"We're missing something," I told Dastrie when we finally reached our suite. "I feel it—but I don't know what it is."

The East Coast contingent of The Phantom Detective Agency was waiting for us, together with our friends among the Little People, and we brought them up-to-date on the most recent developments.

"Ideas, anyone?" I asked.

I looked around at their tired, worried faces, but no one was talking.

And then Belle Darling finally said: "You know, it's kinda like a magic trick."

"What do you mean?" Dastrie asked.

"Well, it just seems to me, Darling [she pronounced it 'Dawlin'], that all this time this Petey Souris—the Little Mouse—has been playing you, just like magicians do on stage—or that ventriloquist that he worked with. Everything they do is supposed to distract the audience from what's really going on—to fool them—and he's doing the same thing with you. That's the world he came from. That's how he thinks, Sweetie.

"He does one big thing for y'all to focus on, so you don't see what he's really doing—until it's too late. And then he's gone—poof!—just like that! It's the oldest trick in the book."

"She's right!" Dastrie said. "She's absolutely right! At every stage in this charade we've been following along in this man's footsteps, always running to catch up. But he's been moving all of us around like pawns on a chessboard. What do we actually know about him? Not much, really. We don't know why he's doing this. We need to focus on the things that we *do* know.

"For example, we know that Smith was associated with the Fraternal Rotary of Gnomes. He directed the headquarters in Harlem, which is now destroyed, but we also saw him at another facility...."

"...Santy's Village!" everyone chimed in.

"Yes! When we visited there, Madame Doyenne went out of her way to show us everything we wanted to see. Nothing was hidden. Everything was *exactly* what it appeared to be—too exactly, now that I think about it. Maybe *nothing* was quite what it seemed.

"The Village operates as a commercial enterprise to hide the activities of Smith and his cronies. *That's* why he was there: to make sure we didn't see more than we were supposed to see. That's why Cohn was there too! And that's where he'll be tomorrow."

"What time does Santy's Village close on Christmas Eve?" I asked.

"Eight o'clock," Yulie said.

"Then I think it's time to pay Old Saint Nick another visit before he hitches up his reindeer tonight."

* * * * * * *

I rented a bus to transport us to Ronkonkoma. In addition to the members of our agency, we had the support of fifty of the Little People, secured through the aegis of the King of the Gnomes.

"We must be a part of this," John Ball had said—and who was I to deny someone of the royal blood?

We reached the town at nine o'clock, and headed down the lonely road to Santy's Village, which was almost deserted at this time of night. I had the driver pull into a park a few hundred feet short of the entrance, and we quietly and carefully debarked.

"If you're threatened," I said, as everyone gathered 'round, "Shoot at the torsos of the Nasty Gnomes. They'll be wounded, but not fatally so. We want to give them a chance eventually to recover their health and sensibilities."

And then we headed out. There were only a few cars scattered throughout the parking lot—I saw a Nash, a Studebaker, a Ford, a Dodge, and several beat-up old semis. The main building was all aglimmer with Christmas lights, but the other structures on the property had gone dark. I motioned for everyone else to stay back, while I walked boldly up to the front door.

I pounded several times, but there was no response. The outside ticket booth was dark and empty. I tried turning the main door handle, and the knob moved without resistance. I cracked open the entrance and peered inside—the hall was vacant. I waved to the others to join me, and then quietly slipped inside. The fireplace was filled with brightly burning logs that had evidently been placed there fairly recently.

"Where *is* everybody?" Dastrie hissed in my right ear, causing me to jump almost out of my skin.

"Don't *do* that!" I said. My heart was racing.

I sent my minions off to explore the open doorways, checking for possible residents—and also dispatched a four-man crew upstairs.

"Nothing!" each group reported back in succession. *"Nothing!"*

"Spread out to either side of the room," I ordered them, and they moved right and left to line the walls. I wanted to view the hall in its entirety—I remembered what Belle Darling had said about Petite Souris's habit of misdirection.

And then I saw it! There was a slight scrape right in the middle of the place, maybe twenty feet in front of the main stairwell. It led off to one side, to the very center of the fireplace.

I walked over to the huge open maw of the pit, until the heat of the blaze forced me to stop. The flickering light generated by the flames made it difficult to see the frame surrounding the fireplace. I grabbed a metal poker from its rack, and used it to bang slightly on the wall next to the brick structure. When I sensed an odd reverberation, I tried prying the thing into the place where the frame met the wall. I did this for several minutes, moving it up and down the edge of the thing, until suddenly I heard an audible "click."

I stepped back as the entire fireplace pivoted outwards into the room. Inside was a stone stairwell leading down into the darkness, dimly lighted by a string of bare bulbs tacked to the ceiling. I pulled out my automatic, and motioned for my companions to follow me into the depths.

Somewhere in the distance I could hear the "boom-boom-boom" of a machine, perhaps, or some very loud music. Step by step we descended beneath the great lodge, until we finally emerged at the mouth of a tunnel extending both right and left. Since the booming noise was coming from the right, that's where I ventured, my crew dutifully following along behind me.

We must have gone at least a hundred yards—well beyond the building itself—when we came to a set of large bronze doors, intricately etched with motifs from some ancient mythology. Giant animals, grotesque gods, ghastly shaped gnomes of various sizes—they were all intertwined in some kind of a bizarre menagerie.

"The Temple of Rübezahl, Lord of the Mountains!" Yulie exclaimed. "I'd thought this no more than a fiction, but now...."

The throbbing came from within. I grabbed one of the great brass knockers in my hand and pulled—and just like the huge fireplace, the door moved quite easily on its pivot, although it must have weighed tons.

The sound was overwhelming: it permeated both body and mind, making ordinary conversation impossible. I didn't recognize the instruments, if that's what they were. Intermingled among the weirdness of the tones was a constant banging of what sounded like metal on metal.

Down in the center of the amphitheater I saw an immense pit of fire, roaring with flames, occasionally spitting orange fireballs into the air. The bare stone seats, carved right out of the underlying rock, were filled with the Nasty Gnomes, intently watching the drama being played out down below.

And it *was* a drama, I gradually realized, a presentation that included both male and female performers dressed in strange costumes from early German or Norse mythology.

"What is this?" I shouted into Yulie's ear.

"The *Unterzwerges*," he said, "The Cavern Dwarves. In the old stories, they're the slaves of the Gnome King."

"What are they doing down there?" I yelled.

"According to ancient legend, they were enthralled by Rübezahl to create the weapon through which he would conquer the Upper-World—our world—of man. It took the shape of a great spear—the *Feuerlanze* or 'Fire Lance'—that would give the gnomes hegemony over both the upper and lower worlds. The weapon could only be fashioned from a special metal that had fallen out of the sky."

"A meteorite."

"Perhaps. As I say, it was an old tale. I never gave it much credence until now."

We crept closer to the top edge of the basin, where we could better view what was occurring down below. Now I could see teams of the gnarly gnomes wielding great mallets in tandem, each striking a long shaft of some weirdly hued ore as it was systematically shifted back and forth over the fire pit. Bang, bang, bang, they went, and with each swing of their sledgehammers, they sent sparks flying in every direction. Some of the creatures pounding on the structure were the largest specimens of the Nasty Gnomes that I'd ever seen, almost as big as normal-sized men.

"The Energizer: it works!" John Ball exclaimed.

"But at what cost?" I muttered.

Then I spotted Smith, clothed in furs and wearing a helmet sprouting two horns. He was off to one side, directing the creation of the weapon and the stoking of the flames.

"Sacrilege!" the King exclaimed. "He has no right!"

And before I could do anything to stop him, John Ball dashed down a nearby aisle, heading right for the pit. I hurried along behind him, his sister and Yulie following me.

Smith spotted him halfway down the side of the amphitheater, and immediately ordered his minions to cease their labor. Everything suddenly went quiet, except for the continual roaring of the flames.

When Ball reached the floor, he turned and faced the Nasty Gnomes, with his own men now surrounding the uppermost of the stone galleries, and shouted: "I am Zähler, true King of the Gnomes, chosen by them in lawful Assembly. This imposter has assumed my title and my trappings. I challenge him to the fire-death. Let him come forward, or let him be called what he is: a thief and a liar."

Smith stepped out where he could be seen. "I am Rübezahl, true King of the Gnomes. The Ancient Gods have blessed me with the secret of augmentation. Only I have the power to increase your size. This *midget* is the imposter. I accept his challenge."

Then I heard a rumbling deep within the earth, and I realized after a moment that I was hearing the chorus of gnomes shouting for their champions.

"Do you really want to do this?" I asked John Ball.

"I have no choice. It's the only way to stop the killing. If I win, they'll follow me. If I lose, well, we're all dead anyway."

He began stripping off his clothing, until he was down to a pair of underpants.

"Help me put this on," he said, as one of the gnomes brought him a jar of some brown greasy substance. It smelled like rancid animal fat.

Yulie and I rubbed it all over the King while a structure was being erected behind me; Smith's supporters were doing the same to him. Then each contestant strapped thick wooden shoes over their feet, and heavy pads to their knees and elbows.

When I turned around, I realized that the gnomes had raised the framework that had held the *Feuerlanze*, and then laid a bare metal plank across the top.

When everything was ready, the contestants were boosted to either end of the new shelf. The fire had died down a bit, but was still fiercely hot over the center of the pit. The radiated heat had already raised enough sweat to soak right through my winter clothing.

"Let the Big Person serve as arbiter," Smith suggested, smiling his crooked smile at me.

"Agreed," John Ball said.

"What does that mean?" I asked.

"You will decide when the contest will pause so that both combatants can refresh themselves. You will adjudicate any fouls. You will decide when the struggle is over."

"When does the fight end?"

"When one of the challengers is dead."

And then it started.

It reminded me of a wrestling match. Each combatant grabbed the other, and tried to push his opponent off the plank and into the pit. However, the grease made their limbs slippery and hard to handle. As the match progressed, the piece of metal on which the pair was perched gradually began to heat up, and soon they were fighting the fire as much as each other. Their clogs began to smoke beneath their feet.

"Yield," Smith yelled, "and I will be merciful."

The King said nothing, but continued to struggle against his younger challenger. Then Ball slipped and fell to one knee. I could tell from the grimace on his face that the metal was searing his calf. Smith grabbed the monarch's upper torso and tried to flip him over the edge, but had a hard time getting a grip. The King suddenly used the leverage from his burning leg to boost Petite Souris right up into the air—Smith bounced once off the edge of the metal plank, and then rolled off into the pit.

He screamed briefly.

"Ohhhh," the gnomes moaned—and they suddenly rose up and began pounding the stone seats with their feet. The King was lifted down from his perch, where he was tended by the Queen his sister. Then he stood up, hobbling a bit.

"I am Zähler, true King of the Gnomes!" he said. "You will follow me and obey!"

And wonder of wonders, they did!

CHAPTER TWELVE

A VISIT FROM ST. NICHOLAS
▲
Happy Christmas to all, and to all a good night!
—Clement Clarke Moore
▼

NEW YORK, NEW YORK
FRIDAY, 25 DECEMBER 1953

We spent most of the night at Santy's Village, trying to sort out the mess we'd made. The first thing I did was to telephone Fast Eddie Underhill; he made the necessary connections with the local constabulary, and also appeared himself on site within a few hours.

"Well, this kinda lassos everythin' up into a pretty neat package," he said. "We've taken custody of all the remainin' 'gnombres,' and we're puttin' 'em in institutions where they'll be gradually weaned from the drug. The main perp is dead—we'll recover his skeleton when the pit cools down enough. The Mayor is very pleased."

"What about Cohn?" I asked.

"That old outlaw? He wasn't directly involved, was he?"

"There's no evidence tying him specifically to the Nasty Gnomes," I had to admit, "but he did provide funding for the foundation."

"Which also supports Santy's Village and many other good thin's," the former Police Commissioner said. "Van, you just can't go around accusin' someone like Cohn without some hard evidence. And pardner, I just don't see that you have anythin' solid here."

"Maybe not. But I know he was part of this."

"Knowin' and provin' are two different things, *hombre*. Let it go for now."

And then one of the officers called him into another room, and Dastrie and I and the rest of our team were left sitting with our crew in the dining area. John Ball, the King of the Gnomes, and his people were trying to restore order, and planned to remain at the lodge for as long as necessary. Of Madame Doyenne, there was no sign.

I'd already had the place thoroughly searched before the gendarmes had arrived, looking for samples of the Energizer and any of the papers relating to its development. We did locate a laboratory in another of the underground hideaways that had been chewed out of the earth beneath Santy's Village, but there wasn't much left there, other than one container of the drug. Indeed, everything seemed almost sparkling clean—too clean, if you know what I mean!

"There has to be another facility somewhere else," Dastrie said. "We only found that lone vat containing the formula, not enough to sustain them for more than a few weeks."

"You're probably right," I said, "but it could be anywhere."

We never did locate a third site, if one even existed.

For now, though, it was time to consider our options. It would be light in a few hours, and we were all exhausted.

"I don't think there's anything else we can do here," I said. "Why don't we head back to town?"

When Fast Eddie returned, I asked permission to leave.

"That's fine," he said, "but you'll have to make formal statements, all of you, within the next few days."

"We can visit Police Headquarters tomorrow," I said.

When we got back to the Big City, I had the driver drop us at the hotel, and then gave him instructions to deliver each of our comrades to wherever they wanted to go.

"Good work, all of you," I said, before they left.

And then Dastrie and I wearily made our way up to our suite.

I'd just opened the door to the inner sanctum when I heard a noise inside. I motioned my wife to keep quiet and pulled out my automatic. I found him sitting in a chair in the kitchen alcove, sipping a cup of hot tea.

"Not bad," he said, when we entered the room.

"What the hell are *you* doing here, Cohn?" I asked. "Don't you have a life?"

"I just wanted to thank you on behalf of the interested parties," he said. "And to answer your question, those of us who labor on behalf of this great country must often sacrifice their personal time to the betterment of the cause."

"Thank me for *what?*"

"For taking care of a mutual problem we shared—and for the additional supply of the drug."

"You mean…?" Dastrie asked. "How did you know?"

"Yes—it's already been confiscated by the government. And yes, Mrs. Van Loan, we do have our sources."

Cohn smiled his crooked grin at us. I almost puked.

"What possible good will the drug do you—or anyone else, for that matter—without knowing how to manufacture it?" I asked.

"Who knows? Maybe we can figure that out for ourselves. We do have a few intelligent folks working for us, after all. But that's not your concern, Mr. Van Loan."

He finished his tea, and very prissily held the empty cup up to the light, looking at the maker's stamp impressed on the bottom.

"Not really quality ware for a hotel of this caliber," he said. "I much preferred the set you had in your old quarters. You know, the Souchon china."

Then he got up, put on his overcoat—all perfectly tailored, of course—straightened his shoulders, and bowed—I swear he bowed.

"Until our next encounter, Mr. and Mrs. Van Loan. In the meantime, happy Christmas to all—and to all a good night!"

He was still ho-ho-hoing as he closed the main door behind him.

"I really hate that smarmy little bastard," Dastrie said. "He's as queer as a three-cent piece."

"Really? I didn't catch that."

"*Really!*" she said. "Take my word for it, Richard. We ladies know these things."

"Hmm. So that's his little secret, eh? I'll have to keep that in mind for the future. Listen, my dear, if I don't get some shut-eye real soon, I may find myself falling into a deep, dark hole somewhere."

We were both too tired by this point to do much of anything but crawl in bed and collapse.

We slept until late that afternoon, and then called down to the kitchen; they'd roasted several turkeys with all the fixings for Christmas, which sounded good enough for the both of us. When the carts arrived, we stuffed ourselves absolutely silly.

"Oh, that tasted so good," Dastrie finally said, burping very daintily. "But I couldn't eat another bite."

"Me either. I guess I'll just have to give you your present now."

Although our living quarters in the Brockleigh-Greeneleaffe Building had been damaged by smoke, they were otherwise intact, and I'd had Moco retrieve the Navajo turquoise and coral necklace that I'd bought her.

"Why, it's simply gorgeous!" she said, putting it around her lovely neck and kissing me. "How did you...?"

"Ah, ve have our vays!" I said.

"Thank you so much, Richard. And now I'm forced to reciprocate, aren't I?"

"I suppose," I said, "although there's really nothing I want more in this world than you."

"Well," she said, "it looks as if you're about to have just that: something more than me."

"What?" I asked.

I couldn't figure it out—and I sure as hell couldn't figure *her* out! She was just sitting there, grinning at me in her very strange, Cheshire cat way.

"I'm pregnant, Richard," she said.

Ho, ho, ho!

EPILOGUE

THE PHANTOM DEPARTURE
▲
"Of shoes—and ships—and sealing wax—
Of cabbages—and kings—."
—Lewis Carroll
▼

San Bernardino, California
25 January 2008

I was sitting in my campus office working on the history of the university when Dastrie Van Loan appeared in the doorway. I recognized her pattern of walking before I even saw her, and invited her into the room without even turning around.

""""The time has come," the Walrus said, "to talk of many things"."" Her soft voice was almost a whisper, a puff of fantasy and nothingness.

"Charles Lutwidge Dodson," I said, speaking over my shoulder, "better known as Lewis Carroll. Are you Alice?"

"Wrong piece," she said. "In any case, I have always been my own sculptress."

"So you and Richard had a child," I said, changing the subject.

"We did," she admitted. "But that's another story, and not one that I want to talk about today. We did so many things together before that final separation."

"I was wondering about that," I said, finally turning 'round in my old, beat-up swivel chair. "You never told me when Richard died."

"No, I didn't." She planted her still-svelte frame in one of my guest seats, right next to the small bamboo in the Chinese pot, and crossed her legs. She picked up the framed photograph of my daughter, Louise. "Pretty girl," she said, and put it back down again.

138

"Yes, she is. I was surprised that someone like Cohn was involved in *The Nasty Gnomes* affair."

"Mr. Cohn had his greasy fingers stuck in many different pies. He was an ambitious man utterly without moral principles, and that made him a dangerous adversary. This was just the first time we encountered him. There were other occasions, as you shall see."

"One thing I don't understand," I said, "is where Smith got the notion that Richard was involved in his father's death. No one apparently knew about that except The Phantom himself."

"He figured it out on his own—or perhaps he guessed. He'd been told by his mother that Peter Maussey *Senior* had been responsible for the deaths of Richard's parents, and he put himself in Richard's place. He simply extrapolated what he might have done under similar circumstances—and he was right, of course. But there was no proof.

"In any case, I'm not sure he really cared all that much about his so-called revenge: he didn't have those kinds of feelings for other people. You have to love passionately to hate passionately. It was just a convenient excuse to involve Richard in an extortion scheme."

"So you're satisfied with the manuscript as submitted?" I asked.

"More or less. You paint a very dark picture of my husband."

"'I paint what I see,' to quote Gahan Wilson. Richard Curtis Van Loan wasn't always a nice man. He had thorns. Decades of fighting crime behind the scenes had warped his character, and he knew this himself. It's a tribute to the essential honesty and decency of the man that he was able to break out of his shell long enough to establish a relationship with another person."

"It wasn't always fun and games between us," she admitted. "But we did love each other, and that helped smooth over the rough patches. Again—as you shall see."

"Why me?"

She laughed out loud. "Your great-uncle...."

"Great-uncle, schmunkle," I said. "Don't give me that bullshit, Ms. Van Loan. I've been wondering for quite some time whether my great-uncle was really Richard Curtis Van Loan."

Silence filled the corners of my office, slowly permeating the fossils, real and perceived, filling the buggy corpses mounted in their plastic display cases, and impressing itself upon the Greek, Roman, and Indic pottery.

"This place is almost a museum," she noted, looking for the first time at the many curios I'd collected. "*You're* almost a museum, Professor Simmons."

I chuckled a few times.

"The thought has occurred to me," I said. "You have a way of not answering my questions that's very charming. If I were twenty years older...."

"You'd do what?" she said. "You still wouldn't be my match, and you know it! Richard and I were two of a kind. The wonder is that we didn't kill each other at some point. You're just an observer, Dr. Simmons, a little boy watching real people meander through their lives."

"That's what writers do," I said. "We watch, we record, we play with people, and sometimes we invent our own universes. We don't live in the same ways that normal folks do. We create all of you within our mind's eye. And I don't honestly know which is the better course: living well or recording the exploits of others. *You* think you know what's real and what isn't, what's right and what isn't, but you're slumming along with the rest of us, Ms. Van Loan. *I* know that. I believe you do too."

"It's time for me to go, Professor Simmons. I do look forward to our next little literary adventure together. Perhaps I may even find myself lurking there—around some corner!"

Then she fluttered out of my life again, much like the proverbial butterfly, vanishing through my chamber door—and I wondered, not for the first time, whether I was *her* creation—or she *mine*!

AUTHOR'S NOTE

A sequel to a sequel: that was the challenge in writing *The Nasty Gnomes*: creating a story that was interesting for the reader while still finding ways to stretch the character of Richard Curtis Van Loan, the Phantom.

The Phantom's Phantom had redefined Van Loan as a more modern man, an older man, a presumably wiser man who had finally found some answers to the dilemma of his existence as a sometime vigilante crime fighter.

But what else could he be?

In the first book, Richard had found himself a match in Dastrie Lee Underhill, the daughter of a former New York City Police Commissioner. She had soothed the savage beast—or so it had appeared.

On reflection, however, that seemed to me too pat an answer. The demons were still there, somewhere, just under the surface—and they would probably never, ever truly be banished from Van Loan's soul.

To become a killer—even a killer on the side of justice—The Phantom had had to depress and suppress his basic sense of decency. What he was doing was wrong, even if it felt right at times, and he was too intelligent a man not to understand that fact in some basic and vital way. But repressing such emotions is never an answer. They have an unpleasant history of erupting again at the most inopportune times.

Just as the gnomes are coming out of the gutters to plague the metropolis of New York, so the hidden darkness in Richard's soul is crawling its way to the surface, confounding both him and his new wife and their relationship. Thus, the nastiness lies both within and without.

That streak of darkness seemed to me the right way to approach this novel, and once I got into that mode, the book wrote itself. Thus, the second of The Phantom Detective volumes is much more like a 1950s' noir mystery than the first. I have enough dark corners in my own mind that finding connections with Van Loan's character was fairly easy.

And New York seemed to me a potentially darker setting than sunny Southern California, where the action of *The Phantom's Phantom* took place. Big cities have lots of crusty, cruddy undercurrents, places and people who can be counted on to be venial, vicious, and vile.

I have deliberately smudged the map of the Big Apple in the 1950s. Actual districts are mentioned in passing, and the geography is more or less correct, but no real structures are involved in the action. You will look in vain for the Brockleigh-Greeneleaffe Building, or even for Santy's Village in Ronkonkoma.

I also took the lives of the Little People in vain, for which my profound apologies. I tried to give them the same complement of heroes and villains that the Big People have, for they are neither better nor worse than the enemy that is ultimately "us."

1953 was a time of transition in America. General Dwight D. Eisenhower had just become president. Senator Joseph McCarthy had reached the peak of his communist-scavenging hate-mongering. The Korean War had finally finished—yet unfinished! And I was then living in the little town of Fairview, Massachusetts; I remember those days of my youth through rose-colored glasses, but I and my dear old mother are the only ones left who do.

This is my eighth novel, and will probably be my 113th published book when it finally appears. Each seems a miracle to me as it's born. Thanks once again to my agent, Shawna McCarthy (no relation to Joe!); to John Gregory Betancourt, my publisher; and to my own Dastrie Lee, my wife Mary—my editor, my companion, my life.

—Robert Reginald
San Bernardino, California
25 January 2008

ABOUT THE AUTHOR

ROB REGINALD was born in Japan in the Year of the Rat, and lived in Turkey as a youth. He starting writing as a mere child, and penned his first book during his senior year in college. He's been infected with terminal logorrhea ever since, churning out twelve million words of professional fiction and nonfiction. He settled in Southern California many, many moons ago, where he worked as an academic librarian for thirty-five years, in addition to grinding out more volumes than anyone would ever care to find, much less read. He's now officially retired—and working harder than ever. In his spare time he edits a line of books for the Borgo Press Imprint of Wildside Press. He loves to hear from his readers. His website can be found at:

www.millefleurs.tv

Printed in the United States
130729LV00003B/1-12/P